Judy Blume spent her childhood in Elizabeth, New Jersey, making up stories inside her head. She has spent her adult years in many places, doing the same thing, only now she writes her stories down on paper. More than 80 million copies of her books have been sold, and her work has been translated into thirty-one languages. She receives thousands of letters every month from readers of all ages, who share their feelings and concerns with her.

In 1996 Judy was honoured by the American Library Association with the Margaret A. Edwards Award for Lifetime Achievement. In 2004 she received the National Book Foundation's Medal for Distinguished Contribution to American Literature.

Judy lives on islands up and down the east coast of America with her husband. They have three grown-up children and one grandchild.

Judy says, 'The best books come from somewhere deep inside. You don't write because you want to, but because you *have* to.'

For more information visit Judy's website:
www.judyblume.com

JUDY BLUME

BLUME

Starring

SALLY J. FREEDMAN

AS HERSELF

MACMILLAN CHILDREN'S BOOKS

in association with Heinemann

First published in the UK 1983 by William Heinemann Ltd

This edition published 2011 by Macmillan Children's Books
a division of Macmillan Publishers Limited
20 New Wharf Road, London N1 9RR
Basingstoke and Oxford
Associated companies throughout the world
www.panmacmillan.com

ISBN 978-1-4472-0287-5

A CIP catalogue record for this book is available from
the British Library.

Printed and bound by CPI Group (UK) Ltd, Croydon CR0 4YY

For my favourite aunt, Frances Goldstein
. . . who is also my friend

Introduction

When World War II ended I was just seven years old, but the war had so coloured my early life that it was hard to think of anything else. No one I knew had actually experienced the war first hand. There were no bombs dropped on America; we were not starving; we felt reasonably safe. And yet I could not help worrying that it could happen again, could happen to us. I knew that Adolf Hitler was a menace. I knew that he wanted to kill all the Jews in the world. And I was a Jew.

Starring Sally J. Freedman As Herself is my most autobiographical novel. Sally is the kind of child I was, full of imagination, always making up stories inside her head. In a way I think the character of Sally explains how and perhaps why I became a writer. My love of storytelling, although I didn't necessarily share it in those days, has carried through to today.

Some of the Yiddish expressions used by Sally's grandmother in the book are words I learned from my own grandmother. Sally's family is based on my own. And the setting, Miami Beach, Florida, in 1947–48, is real too. I spent two school years living in Miami Beach after the war. Sally's world is the world as I perceived it, at age ten. A world full of secrets, full of questions that no one would answer.

I hope that you can put yourselves into post-war

America and enjoy reading about Sally and her family. Sally is one of my favourite characters. I hope she'll become one of yours, too.

Judy Blume

Prologue

'Can I have another jelly sandwich?' Sally asked her grandmother, Ma Fanny. They were in the kitchen of the rooming house, sitting on opposite sides of the big wooden table.

'Such big eyes!' Ma Fanny said, laughing. 'You still have half a sandwich left.'

'I know, but it's so good!' Sally licked the jelly from the corners of her mouth. 'I could eat twenty sandwiches, at least.'

'Only twenty?'

'Maybe twenty-one,' Sally said. 'Why don't you make yourself a jelly sandwich, too . . . and if you can't finish it, I will.'

'I should eat jelly and have heartburn all night?' Ma Fanny asked.

'Jelly gives you heartburn?'

'I'm sorry to say . . .' Ma Fanny turned on the radio. Bing Crosby was singing.

Sally hummed along with him, every now and then singing a line out loud. 'Or would you rather be a horse? A horse is an animal . . .' She wiggled around in her chair. The sand in the bottom of her bathing suit made her itch. Soon she would go upstairs for her bath. Everyone had to sign up for a bath here, because all the guests in the rooming

1

house shared the bathrooms. It was the same with the kitchen. Each family had a shelf in the pantry and space in the icebox, but no one had to sign up to cook.

Upstairs, Sally's family had rented two bedrooms for ten days. One was for Daddy and Mom and the other was for Sally, her brother Douglas, and Ma Fanny. Sally was the youngest so she got to sleep on the cot under the window. From it she could see the organ grinder and his monkey when they were still a block away. She didn't tell this to Douglas because if he had known he would have wanted to sleep on the cot for the rest of their vacation.

'Drink all your milk,' Ma Fanny said, 'and you'll grow up to be a big, strong girl.'

'I already am big and strong,' Sally answered, making a muscle with her arm.

Ma Fanny reached across the table and squeezed Sally's arm. 'Hoo hoo . . . that's *some* muscle!'

'So can I have another jelly sandwich?'

'Such a one-track mind,' Ma Fanny said, laughing again. She tapped her fingers on the table, keeping in time to the tune on the radio.

Mrs Sternberger, another guest in the rooming house, swept into the kitchen. She took a dish of rice pudding from the icebox and joined Sally and Ma Fanny at the table. As soon as she sat down she noticed the jar of grape jelly with the cap off. 'What are you doing with my grape jelly?' she asked, picking up the jar.

'It's not yours,' Ma Fanny told her. 'It's mine.'

2

'I just bought this yesterday,' Mrs Sternberger said, replacing the cap. She stood up, holding onto the jar, and pointed at Ma Fanny. 'I knew I couldn't trust you the minute I met you.'

'What are you, crazy?' Ma Fanny asked, raising her voice. 'I should use your grape jelly when I have my own? I wouldn't touch yours with a ten-foot pole!'

'And I wouldn't believe you for all the tea in China!' Mrs Sternberger answered, angrily.

'So, who asked you?' Ma Fanny turned to Sally. 'Would you like another jelly sandwich, sweetie pie?'

'Sure.' Sally was surprised that Ma Fanny had changed her mind.

Ma Fanny reached for the jelly jar but Mrs Sternberger said. 'Not with *my* grape jelly!' She held it to her chest.

'Oh . . . go soak your head!' Ma Fanny said.

'Go soak your own!'

Sally wanted to laugh but knew that she shouldn't. 'Can I please have my sandwich?' She shouted to make sure she was heard.

Suddenly, Bing Crosby stopped singing. 'We interrupt this programme to bring you a bulletin from our newsroom,' the announcer said. 'The war is over!'

Ma Fanny and Mrs Sternberger grew quiet. 'Did I hear what I think I heard?' Mrs Sternberger asked.

'Sha . . .' Ma Fanny said, turning up the volume on the radio. Both women listened carefully.

The announcer repeated the news. '*The war is over!*' His voice broke on the last word.

'Thank God . . . thank God . . .' Ma Fanny cried.

Mrs Sternberger plonked the jar of grape jelly on the table and whooped for joy. She and Ma Fanny hugged and kissed. They began to laugh and cry at the same time. 'It's over . . . it's over . . . it's over!' They danced around the kitchen.

Sally felt alone. She wanted to dance with them. She pushed her chair back and ran to Ma Fanny's side. Ma Fanny and Mrs Sternberger dropped hands to make a circle with Sally, and the three of them danced. 'The war is over . . . over . . . over . . .' Sally sang.

The other guests in the rooming house joined them. Daddy and Mom and Douglas were there. It was like a party. A very tall man named Ben held Sally up in the air and twirled around and around with her until she felt dizzy and begged him to put her down.

That night they all marched on the boardwalk, waving small American flags. Daddy carried Sally on his shoulders. He stopped at a stand to buy horns for her and Douglas to toot. Sally's throat felt sore, maybe from cheering so loud.

Douglas said, 'Hey, Dad . . . when we get home can I have your air raid helmet?'

'I don't see why not, son,' Daddy said.

'Won't there be any more blackouts?' Sally asked.

'No, dummy,' Douglas said, 'the war is over!'

'I know that!' But Sally didn't know that meant the end of blackouts. So now Daddy wouldn't patrol the streets any more, wearing his white air raid helmet. And she and Douglas wouldn't get into bed with Mom, waiting for Daddy to come home, telling them it had just been practice, that the war was far, far away and nothing bad was ever going to happen to them.

'I'd like your helmet, too,' Sally said. How was she supposed to know that Daddy would be giving it away now?'

'Not fair!' Douglas said. 'I'm older.'

'Tell you what . . .' Daddy said, 'you can *share* it.'

'Her head's so little it'll cover her whole face,' Douglas said.

'Little heads are better than big ones,' Sally told him.

'Children . . . *please* . . .' Mom said.

Daddy put Sally down and went off to sing with a group of men. Sally took Mom aside and said, 'I don't feel so good.'

'What is it?' Mom asked, looking concerned.

'My throat hurts . . . and my stomach feels funny.'

Mom touched Sally's forehead. 'You don't feel warm . . . it's probably all the excitement.'

'I don't think so,' Sally said, 'I feel sick.'

'Let's stay out a little while longer . . . it's warm enough . . . I'm sure you won't get a chill . . .' Mom took Sally's hand.

'But Mom . . .'

'Try not to think about it,' Mom said. 'Tonight is special.'

'I know, but . . .'

'Think about peace instead . . . think about Uncle

5

Jack coming home . . . think about Tante Rose and Lila . . .'

'Who are they?'

'You know . . . Ma Fanny's sister and her daughter . . . my *Aunt* Rose and my *cousin*, Lila . . .'

'Oh, them . . . the ones Hitler sent away . . .'

'Yes. Maybe now we can find out where they are.'

'Do you think they're in New Jersey?' Sally asked.

'No, honey . . . they're far away . . . they're some-where in Europe.'

'Oh . . . my throat still hurts bad.'

'Please, Sally,' Mom said, 'try for me . . .'

Sally tried to think of other things, as her mother said. She kept marching even though she felt worse and worse. Finally, she couldn't wait any more. 'Mom . . . I think I'm going to . . .' She ran to the side of the boardwalk, leaned over the rail and threw up on to the beach.

'Oh, honey . . . I'm sorry,' Mom said. 'I should have listened.' She wiped Sally's mouth with a Kleenex. 'Don't cry . . . it's all right . . .'

'I didn't mess myself up,' Sally said, sniffling. 'See . . . I was really careful, wasn't I?'

'Yes, you were.'

'I knew you wouldn't want me to get it on my dress.'

'That's right . . . it's just as easy to be careful . . .'

They went back to the rooming house and Mom took Sally's temperature. It was 103°. She put Sally to bed, gave her some ginger ale to sip and laid a cold, wet wash-cloth on her forehead. 'If only I had listened when you first told me you weren't feeling well . . . I was so excited myself . . . I . . .' She kissed Sally's cheek. 'Try and get to sleep . . . tomorrow we'll go to the doctor . . .' Mom pulled a chair up to Sally's cot and sat beside her. Sally closed her eyes and listened to the sounds outside. Cheering, horns tooting, singing . . . laughter . . . sounds of the celebration. Slowly, she drifted off to sleep.

Chapter 1

Sally had a scab on her knee from falling off her bicycle last week. It itched. She scratched the area around it, knowing that the scab wasn't ready to come off yet. She was sitting on the high-backed chair near the fireplace and her feet didn't quite reach the floor. She wished they would.

'Little pitchers have big ears,' Uncle Jack said, with a nod in her direction. On the far side of the living-room Mom, Ma Fanny, Aunt Bette and Uncle Jack were huddled together. They spoke in hushed voices so that Sally could make out only a few words.

'God forbid . . . keep your fingers crossed . . . never should have gone there . . .'

They were talking about Douglas. Something had happened to him. Sally wasn't exactly sure what, but Daddy was at the hospital now, with Douglas, and Mom was waiting impatiently for the phone to ring, with news about him.

Sally ran her hands along the arms of the chair. It was covered in pink and green flowered material, shiny and almost new. The whole living-room was pink and green although Mom didn't say *pink*. She said *rose-beige*. It was a beautiful room, soft and peaceful. Sally loved it. She wished they used it every day and not just on special occasions.

One Sunday her father built a fire in the brick

9

fireplace and he and Sally and Douglas sat around on the floor reading the funnies. But Mom said it made a mess. So they'd had no more log fires. On either side of the fireplace bookcases climbed to the ceiling and between them, and over the fireplace, was a large mirror, reflecting the rest of the room.

Something had to be very wrong with Douglas. Otherwise why were they sitting in the living-room tonight?

'Stop picking, Sally . . .' Mom said. 'You'll only make it worse.'

Sally took her hand away from her knee. She twirled a strand of hair around her finger and yawned.

'Why don't you go up to bed?' Mom asked. 'Look how tired you are.'

'I'm not tired.'

'Don't give me a hard time,' Mom snapped. 'Just go on up . . .'

Aunt Bette touched Mom's shoulder, then walked over to Sally. 'Come on,' she said. 'I'll keep you company while you get ready.'

They went upstairs to Sally's room. Aunt Bette flopped across the bed. She was Mom's younger sister. She taught fourth grade and sometimes she brought marbles to Sally and Douglas, marbles that had wound up in her Treasure Chest because someone in her class had been fooling around with them instead of paying attention. And once a marble found its way into Aunt Bette's Treasure Chest the owner could kiss it goodbye. That's why Douglas and Sally had such great marble collections. Sally's favourite was clear green all over.

'Mom's mad at me,' Sally said, 'and I didn't do anything.'

'She's not mad,' Aunt Bette said. 'She's worried about Douglas, that's all.'

'She acted mad . . . she didn't have to holler.'

'Try to understand.'

'What's the matter with Douglas, anyway?'

'He's had an accident.'

Sally knew that. She'd been outside tossing her pink Spalding ball against the side of the house when two boys carried Douglas to the back door. There'd been a big commotion then and Sally was sure of just one thing. Douglas was crying. She'd been surprised about that.

'They were playing in Union Woods,' Aunt Bette said, 'and Douglas tried to jump across the brook but he lost his balance and fell and when he did he dislocated his elbow.'

'We're not supposed to play in Union Woods,' Sally said. There was a strange man who hung out in there. Last month the principal of Sally's school had sent a notice to each classroom, warning the kids not to go into Union Woods anymore. That afternoon Sally had asked Douglas, 'Do you know about the strange man in Union Woods?' and Douglas had answered, 'Sure.'

'What kind of strange man is he?' Sally said.

'What do you mean?' Douglas asked.

'Is he a murderer or a kidnapper or what?'

'He's just strange,' Douglas told her.

'What does that mean?'

'You know . . .'

'No, I don't!'

'Well . . . he's kind of crazy,' Douglas said.

'Oh, crazy.' Sally thought about that for a minute. 'Crazy how?'

'In general,' Douglas said.

'What does that mean?'

'I don't have time to explain now . . . I'm busy . . .' and before Sally could ask another question Douglas had run downstairs to his basement workshop and shut the door.

Sally supposed Douglas and his friends weren't afraid to go into Union Woods because they were older. They were thirteen and went to junior high. 'Is it bad to dislocate your elbow?' Sally asked Aunt Bette.

'It's like breaking your arm . . . he'll have a cast when he comes home from the hospital.'

'Like Suzanne Beardsley?'

'I don't know her.'

'She's in my class. She broke her wrist taking out the milk bottles and she had a cast for two months and we all signed our names on it.'

'I'm sure Douglas will let you sign your name on his cast too. Now brush your teeth and hop into bed. It's past ten.'

'Can I listen to my radio?'

'Okay . . . but just for a little while.'

Sally got ready for bed. Her mother came up to

12

kiss her goodnight. 'I didn't mean to scold you,' she said. 'It's just that . . .'

'I know,' Sally said, 'you're worried about Douglas.'

'Well, yes . . . waiting is very hard. I should have gone to the hospital too.'

'Will Douglas be home soon?'

'I hope so. Daddy's going to call as soon as his arm is reset.'

'Reset?'

'Yes . . . to get the elbow back in place.'

'Oh.'

'Good night . . . sleep tight.' Mom bent over to kiss her cheek and Sally could smell the pot roast they'd had for dinner on her hands.

'Night, Mom.'

Sally closed her eyes but she couldn't fall asleep. Even her radio didn't help, so after a while she reached over and turned it off. Then she arranged her covers in just the right way, with both her hands tucked inside, and she closed her eyes again, but still, sleep wouldn't come. So she made up a story inside her head.

Sally Meets the Stranger

Sally is walking in Union Woods, picking flowers and humming a tune. She is wearing a long yellow organdie dress and a picture hat to match. Her hair is blowing in the breeze. Suddenly, she is aware of someone following her. She spins around and comes face to face with the strange man. He has a long, shaggy grey beard and a foolish smile on his face. Saliva trickles out of the corners of his mouth. His clothes are tattered and his bare feet are crusted with dirt.

Oh! Sally exclaims and she drops her flowers. The strange man makes terrible noises and Sally tries to run but finds she can't. Her feet won't move. The strange man comes closer and closer. Sally takes off her hat and swats his face with it but since it is made of organdie it doesn't do any good. He scoops her up and carries her deep into Union Woods.

You're going to be very sorry! Sally tells him, as he prepares to tie her to a tree. He answers, *Ugr harmph vilda phud*, then laughs as he winds the rope tighter and tighter around Sally's small body.

But he is *so* strange he forgets to tie the two ends of the rope together and as soon as he goes back to his hut Sally wiggles free and runs. She doesn't stop until she reaches police headquarters, where she tells her story to the Chief of Police himself. Then she leads him and two of his assistants to the strange man's hut. The strange man is captured at last! Never again will he be able to tie a girl to a tree.

The Chief of Police is so impressed that he makes Sally his number one detective, specializing in strange cases. A Hollywood producer decides to make a movie of Sally's story. But he can't find the right ten-year-old girl to play the lead. He decides he must have Sally herself and that is how Sally gets to be not only a famous detective but also a movie star.

★

Sometime that night Douglas came home from the hospital. Sally woke to her parents' voices. Mom cried, 'His clothes are wet . . . my God, Arnold, he's soaked right through.'

'From the brook,' Daddy said. 'He fell into the brook . . . remember?'

'But the hospital . . .' Mom said. 'How could they have left him in these wet clothes for so long . . . he'll get pneumonia or something . . . I knew I should have gone too.'

Chapter 2

Douglas didn't get pneumonia, he got nephritis, a kidney infection. He was very sick and had to stay in bed. Nobody could prove it came from being wet for such a long time but Sally knew that's what her mother was thinking.

Ma Fanny moved into the spare room to help Mom take care of Douglas. And Aunt Bette came over every day after school. She made charts and taped them to the wall in his room. One to keep track of his medicines, another to record his temperature, and a third, showing how many glasses of water he drank each day. If they added up to a quart or more Mom pasted a gold star on that chart at night. Every Thursday afternoon a lab technician would arrive to take some blood from Douglas's arm. Sally wasn't allowed to watch, although she wanted to very much.

Nobody worried about Douglas missing school because he was a genius. He'd skipped third grade which made him the youngest student in eighth. When he was ten he'd built a radio by himself. There wasn't anything he couldn't fix or make from scratch. Still, Sally was glad she wasn't a genius too because Daddy and Mom were never satisfied with Douglas's report card. He didn't get all A's or even all B's like Sally. And his teachers always said the same thing about him. 'Douglas does not work up to his full potential.'

The weather was hot and sticky that May. After school Sally and her best friend, Christine, played together.

'Why can't I see Douglas?' Christine asked Sally.

'Because my mother doesn't want him to get any new germs.'

'I don't have any new germs and besides, I don't want to touch him or anything . . . I just want to see him.'

'Maybe next week . . . I'm not allowed in there myself.'

'Does he look awful?'

'Sort of . . .'

'Did you sign his cast?'

'Not yet . . . I just told you I'm not allowed to get that close . . . but when I do sign it I'm going to draw a *Kilroy Was Here* picture with my name across the brick wall.'

'Lets play Cowgirl today,' Christine said. 'I'm sick of Detective.'

'But we played Cowgirl yesterday and, besides, I've got this really great detective story ready . . .' Sally said. 'We're after this murderer who cuts people up and stuffs the pieces into brown lunch bags . . . he leaves the bags all over town and the people are really scared . . . this is no ordinary murderer . . . this guy is dangerous.'

'Why do you always get to make up the story?' Christine asked.

'Because I'm good at it,' Sally said. 'I'll be in charge of the case and you can be my assistant . . .'

'You were in charge yesterday,' Christine said.

'That was different . . . that was Cowgirl . . .'

'I'll only play if we can be partners,' Christine said.

'Okay . . . we're partners.'

'Good.'

For a while Douglas seemed to be getting better and they made plans to rent a house at Bradley Beach for the summer. Then he got sick all over again and they cancelled their vacation. Mom and Daddy and Ma Fanny spoke in whispers and Sally began to wonder if Douglas might die. If he did she'd be an only child. She could have his bicycle. It was bigger than hers. But then she'd have to learn to ride a boy's bike.

Anyway, she didn't want him to die. And she knew she shouldn't be thinking that way. God could punish her for such evil thoughts. Besides, if Douglas died it wouldn't be fun like when her aunts and uncles and Granny Freedman had died. After their funerals they'd sat shivah for a week, at Sally's house. It was a Jewish custom, to help the family through those difficult first days following a loved one's death. Sally enjoyed sitting shivah very much. Every afternoon and evening friends and relatives would come to visit, bringing baskets of fruit and homemade cakes and cookies and boxes of candy from Barton's. And they would pinch Sally's cheeks, telling her how much she'd grown since the last funeral. Then they'd all sit around and talk and Mom would serve coffee. And as they left they'd always say, 'We must get together on happier occasions.' But they never did.

It seemed to Sally that somebody in her family was always dying. But they were much older or very sick and she didn't know them well enough to really care. The last time they'd sat shivah was in November when Ma Fanny got a letter telling her that Tante Rose and Lila were dead – killed in one of Hitler's concentration camps. And people who Sally had never seen before came to pay condolence calls. People from the old country, who had known Ma Fanny when she was just a girl, before she sailed to America on the banana boat. People who remembered Tante Rose and Lila.

With Douglas it would be different. It wouldn't be like a party at all. Everyone would cry and they would forget all about her. It would be even worse than now. She wished Douglas would hurry and get well so the family could have some time for her too.

When school ended Sally was sent to Day Camp at the Y. And in August Douglas was well again. Towards the end of the month Mom said, 'Daddy and I are going away for a few days.'

'Where to?' Sally asked. 'Bradley Beach?'

'No . . . Florida . . . Ma Fanny will take care of you and Douglas while we're gone.'

'But suppose Douglas gets sick again?'

'He won't . . . the doctor says he's doing fine and we'll just be gone a week . . . maybe less.'

'How will you get there?'

'On the train.'

'But Florida's very far, isn't it?'

'It's a day and a half on the train.'

Sally thought she might start to cry but she wasn't sure why.

'Don't look like that,' Mom said, putting an arm around her. 'Everything's going to be fine . . . and when we come home we may have a big surprise for you.'

'What kind of surprise?'

'If I tell you then it won't be a surprise.'

'Tell me anyway . . . please . . .'

'Can you promise to keep a secret?'

'I promise . . .'

'You won't tell *anybody*?'

Sally shook her head.

'Well . . . Daddy and I are going to look for an apartment in Miami Beach and if we find one then maybe we'll spend next winter there . . . and wouldn't that be fun?'

'You mean all of us?'

'You and Douglas and Ma Fanny and me . . . Daddy would have to stay at home to work, of course . . .'

'But what about school?'

'You'd go to school there . . . wouldn't that be exciting?'

'I don't know.'

'The doctors think it would be very good for

20

Douglas . . . and you always have sore throats in the winter . . . so it would be good for you too.'

'Sometimes I get sore throats in the summer . . . remember the night the war was over . . . remember how my throat hurt then?'

'Yes, but winter is worse . . . and we don't want Douglas to be sick anymore, do we?'

'You just said he's fine.'

'He's getting better . . .'

'You said *fine*.'

'I meant the infection is clearing up . . . but Douglas is very run-down . . . he's lost a lot of weight . . . you can see his ribs . . .'

'You always could.'

'But now you can count them . . . he needs time to recuperate . . .'

'I'm not sure I want to go.'

'Well . . . nothing's definite . . . we'll just see what happens, okay?'

'Okay.'

Sally and her friends were in the playhouse in Sally's backyard. It wasn't a baby kind of playhouse for dolls. It was a big sturdy house that her father and Douglas had built. It was painted white with green shutters. Inside there was a table, four chairs, a built-in wooden bed and three windows. There was a Dutch door, too.

Alice Ingram, who had a recreation room and four telephones at her house, didn't have anything to compare with Sally's playhouse. Alice and Christine were both in Sally's class at school. They sat next to each other on the wooden bed. Betsy, who lived across the street, was a year younger than the other girls but two heads taller. She sat on one of the chairs.

'Let's play Love and Romance today,' Alice said. 'Sally and Betsy can be the boys and me and Christine will be the girls.'

'No, thank you,' Betsy said. 'I was the boy last time.'

'That's because you're so tall,' Christine told her. 'You make a good boy.'

'Let's play War instead,' Sally suggested.

'Oh, I'm sick of playing War,' Alice said. 'I always end up being Hitler!'

'Well, you can't expect me to be Hitler,' Sally said. 'I'm Jewish.'

'So . . . everybody expects me to be the boy and I'm really a girl,' Betsy argued.

'That's different!' Sally said. 'But if you don't want to play War I have another idea . . .'

'What?' Alice Ingram asked.

'We can play Concentration Camp instead. And nobody has to be Hitler because he is away on business.'

'How do you play?' Betsy asked.

'The usual way . . .' Sally answered. 'First I tell you who you are and then I make up the story . . . Alice, you can be Lila . . .'

'Who's she?' Alice asked.

22

'This beautiful woman who gets captured and sent to Dachau.'

'What's that?' Alice asked.

'It's the concentration camp where the story takes place.'

'And Betsy, you can be Tante Rose, Lila's mother . . .'

'Why should I have to be Alice's mother . . . I'm younger . . .'

'Because you're taller . . . now just shut up and listen . . .'

'I don't see why we always have to play Sally's stories,' Betsy whined.

'Because she's good at making them up,' Christine said. 'And besides, it's *her* playhouse.'

'I'll play,' Alice said, 'as long as I can be Lila . . . you did say she was beautiful, didn't you?'

'Yes, very . . . we've got pictures of her. She has long, dark hair and big eyes.'

'Is her mother beautiful too?' Betsy asked.

'Of course. And she's not even *that* old because she had Lila when she was just sixteen.'

'My sister's sixteen,' Betsy said.

'I know . . . I know . . .' Sally was anxious to get on with the game.

'Who am I supposed to be?' Christine asked.

'You can be the concentration camp guard. You hand the pretend soap to Tante Rose and Lila and tell them to go to the showers.'

'Why do they get *pretend* soap?'

'Because it's a trick. They're not really going to

23

get showers, they're going to get killed in a big gas oven.'

'I'm going home,' Betsy said. 'I don't like this game.'

'It is kind of scary,' Christine said. 'I'd rather play Love and Romance.'

'If we do, then I'll stay,' Betsy said.

'Let's take a vote,' Christine said. 'All in favour of Concentration Camp, raise your hands.'

Sally and Alice raised their hands.

'All in favour of Love and Romance, raise yours . . .' Christine and Betsy raised theirs. 'It's a tie.'

'Oh, all right . . .' Sally said, 'we'll play Detective instead. That way nobody wins.'

Later, after Alice and Betsy went home, Christine and Sally sat on the glider swing. 'How long will your parents be in Florida?' Christine asked.

'A week . . . they're looking for an apartment.'

'You're moving?'

'No, silly . . . I'd never move . . . it's just for next winter . . . so Douglas doesn't get sick in the cold weather. And if you tell anybody anything about it I'll kill you . . . it's supposed to be a secret.'

'Who would I tell?'

'I don't know . . . just promise that you won't.'

'Okay . . . I promise . . . I've got to go now . . .'

Sally walked Christine to her bicycle.

'You know who goes to Florida in the winter?' Christine asked.

'No . . . who?'

24

'Millionaires! I read it in my mother's magazine.'
She coasted down Sally's driveway.

'Hey . . . my father's just a dentist,' Sally called,
'not a millionaire . . .'

Christine laughed and waved.

'Hey . . . remember your promise . . . not a word
to anyone.'

'My lips are sealed,' Christine called back.

Bounce . . . catch . . . bounce . . . catch . . . Sally was
tossing her Spalding ball against the side of the house.
The supper that Ma Fanny was cooking smelled
good. Sally guessed it was roast chicken. Bounce . . .
catch . . . bounce . . . catch . . . She had time for just
a short story before Ma Fanny called her in to eat.
At least when she made up the stories inside her
head she didn't have to worry about who would play
what. That was such a waste of time. Let's see, Sally
thought, thinking up a title.

Sally Saves Lila

It is during the war. President Roosevelt asks for
volunteers to go to Europe to help.

Sally is the first on line.

How old are you? the Head of Volunteers asks.

I'm ten, Sally tells her, *but I'm smart . . . and
strong . . . and tough.*

Yes, I can see that, the Head says. *Okay, I'm going
to take a chance and send you . . . your ship leaves in an
hour.*

Thank you, Sally says, *you won't be sorry you chose me.*

Good luck, the Head says.

Sally salutes, slings her duffle bag over her shoulder and boards her ship.

When she arrives in Europe she realizes she had forgotten her toothpaste. She goes into the first Rexall's she sees and selects a tube of Ipana, for the smile of beauty. Then she feels hungry. It must be lunchtime. She finds a deli and orders a salami sandwich on rye and a Coke to go. She takes her lunch to the park across the street and finds a sunny bench. She unwraps her sandwich but before she takes her first bite she hears someone crying.

Sally investigates. After all, she has come to Europe to help. It is a woman, huddled on the ground next to a tall tree. Her hands cover her face, muffling her sobs. She is dressed in rags.

Sally goes to her side. *Are you hungry?* she asks.

The woman does not respond so Sally holds out her sandwich. *It's salami*, she says. *Doesn't it smell good?*

Kosher? the woman asks.

Yes, Sally tells her. *Kosher salami is the only kind I like.*

Me too, the woman says. She reaches for the sandwich and wolfs it down, her back to Sally.

How long has it been since you've eaten? Sally asks.

Days . . . weeks . . . months . . . I don't know anymore.

Where do you live?

I have no home . . . no family . . . no friends . . . all

gone . . . gone . . . Finally she turns around and faces Sally. Even though her hair is filthy and her big eyes are red and swollen and most of her teeth are missing, Sally knows her instantly. *Lila!*

At the sound of her name the woman tries to stand up and run but she is so weak she falls to the ground, beating it with her fists. *I knew you would catch me . . . sooner or later . . . I knew I could never escape . . . but I won't go back to Dachau . . . not ever . . . I'll die right here . . . right now . . .* She pulls a knife from her pocket and aims it at her heart.

No! Sally says, springing to her feet. She wrestles the knife away from Lila. *You don't understand . . . I'm here to help . . .*

You are not with the Gestapo? Lila asks.

No, I'm with the Volunteers of America. I'm Sally J. Freedman, from New Jersey . . . I'm your cousin, once removed . . .

You mean you're Louise's daughter?

Sally nods.

You mean you're Tante Fanny's granddaughter?

Sally nods again.

I can't believe it . . . I can't believe it . . . just when I'd given up all hope. Sally and Lila embrace.

Where's Tante Rose? Sally asks.

Lila begins to cry again. *My mother is dead. We dug the hole together. For five months, every night, we dug the hole . . . until finally it was ready . . . and just when we were going to escape they caught Mama and sent her to the showers. That night I crawled through the hole myself and came out in the forest and I ran and ran and I've been running ever since . . . but not any more . . . I'm too tired . . . too tired to run . . .*

It's all over now, Sally tells Lila. *You're safe. I'm taking you home with me. You can share my room. My father will make you new teeth. He's a very good dentist.*

How can I ever thank you? Lila asks.

Don't even try . . . I'm just doing my job.

The next day, after Lila has a bath and shampoo, a good night's sleep and a big breakfast in bed, she and Sally board the ship for New Jersey. On the way Lila develops a sore throat and a fever of 103°. Sally puts her to bed, gives her ginger ale to sip and keeps a cold cloth on her forehead. She sits at Lila's bedside and tells her stories until Lila is well again.

When they get home Sally is a hero. There is a big parade in her honour on Broad Street and everyone cheers. The people watching from the windows in the office buildings throw confetti, the way Sally did when Admiral Halsey came home at the end of the war.

That night, Sally was soaking in the tub trying to keep cool. When she and Douglas were small they played in the tub together on hot summer days. But Douglas didn't let her see him undressed any more. She lay back in the tub and squeezed her sponge. The water trickled on her legs and belly.

There were four bedrooms in Sally's house but just that one bathroom, unless you counted the one that was off the kitchen, and Sally didn't. That one had only a sink and toilet, while this one had a tub, a separate shower, a hamper, a mirrored cabinet, plus a sink and toilet. The tile was lavender, with black trim. The wallpaper matched and all the wood-work was painted black, including the door. Sally loved it.

Her father didn't. He said it looked like a bordello. 'What's that?' Sally had asked at the time. 'Never mind,' Daddy and Mom had answered together. Then Mom went on to say, 'There's not much you can do with lavender tile, Arnold . . . beside, lavender and black are the newest colours but if you feel that strongly about it we can always rip out the tile and fixtures and start all over . . .' Then Daddy said, 'Hell, no . . . I'll get used to it in time . . . I guess.'

The only thing wrong with the bathroom was you couldn't powder in it because the powder flew all over and made the black woodwork dusty and Mom didn't like that.

The phone rang as Sally was drying herself. If you didn't dry carefully between your toes you could get something called Athlete's Foot and your skin would peel off.

'Sally . . .' Ma Fanny called, 'hurry . . . it's your mother on the line.'

Sally jumped into her robe and dashed to the telephone.

'Hi, honey . . . how're you doing?' Mom asked.

'Okay . . . how's Florida . . . and when are you coming home?'

'Day after tomorrow and it's beautiful!'

'Did you find a place?'

'Yes, just this afternoon.'

'Then we're really going?'

'Most likely ... but the lease isn't signed yet so don't tell anyone.'

'I won't ... I won't ... what's it like?'

'Oh, it's very interesting. How's Douglas?'

'He's fine.'

'Good ... put him on and then you can say hello to Daddy.'

The next day Sally told Christine, 'They found a place. My mother says it's really interesting.'

'When are you going?'

'I don't know ... when it gets cold, I guess ... nothing's definite yet.'

Sally ate lunch at Christine's house. Mrs Mackler made them bologna sandwiches with mayonnaise and lettuce and thick chocolate malteds to drink. Sally wondered if she'd dropped an egg in while they weren't looking the way Ma Fanny did.

Mrs Mackler said, 'I heard you're going to Florida.'

'You did?' Sally gave Christine a *look*.

'Or am I wrong?' Mrs Mackler asked.

'Wrong?'

'Yes, wrong.'

'Well, I don't know ... I don't know anything about any of that.'

'Oh, I see.'

After lunch, when they went outside, Sally told Christine, 'Next time don't *seal* your lips ... *sew* them!'

And Christine said, 'Oh, Sally . . . I only told my mother . . . I can keep a secret as good as you . . . honest!'

Chapter 3

'I had to pay under the table,' Sally's father said, 'but I think it's worth it . . . besides, I had no choice . . . there's so little available.'

They were having Sunday supper at Aunt Bette and Uncle Jack's place, which was over a beauty parlour on the other side of town. Sally tried to picture her father under the table in Miami Beach. Probably the apartment landlord, Mr Koner, was with him. Daddy would take out his money and hand it to Mr Koner. He'd count it, nod, and then they'd both crawl out from under the table together. It didn't make much sense to Sally but she supposed that was the way they did business in Florida.

'Finish the tongue, Sally,' her mother said.

'I'm eating the potato salad first.'

'Finish the tongue, *then* eat the potato salad.'

'Do I have to?'

'You know the poor children are starving in Europe . . . besides, Aunt Bette will be insulted if you don't finish the tongue. She made it herself.'

Aunt Bette was learning to cook now that Ma Fanny, who lived with her and Uncle Jack, was going to Florida. Ma Fanny had always done the cooking. Aunt Bette was gathering recipes on her own these days and trying them out on the family. The tongue was covered with a sweet sauce that had raisins floating in it. Sally couldn't stand the idea of eating some cow's tongue. She looked at Aunt Bette and tried to smile. 'I like the potato salad a lot.'

'Ma Fanny made that,' Aunt Bette said, softly.

'Oh.'

'I'll finish your tongue,' Douglas said. 'I think it's great.'

Aunt Bette beamed.

Sally handed him her plate and was grateful when her aunt changed the subject. 'I still think you should consider getting them there in time to start school,' she told Daddy and Mom. 'It's difficult enough to adjust to a new school situation without coming in mid-term . . .'

'On the other hand,' Daddy said, 'I really don't want them there during the hurricane season . . . it's too risky.'

'So when do you think we should leave?' Mom asked.

'Mid-October . . . that way the danger of the storms will be over and we can still get our money's worth.'

'But we'll come home as soon as winter's over, right?' Sally asked.

'No . . . I think we'll stay and finish the school year,' Mom said. 'Anyway, you'll probably like it so much you'll never want to come home. Just wait till you see those palm trees!'

'But I'll miss Daddy and Aunt Bette and Uncle Jack and Christine and my bed and the bathroom and my other friends and my playhouse and school and . . .'

They all started to laugh. Even Douglas laughed, with his mouth full of food. Sally hated it when the family thought she'd said something funny when she was being serious.

'And I'll miss you, too,' Daddy told her, 'and Douglas and Mom and Ma Fanny . . . but I'll fly down whenever I can.'

'On a plane?' Sally asked.

'He hasn't got wings,' Douglas said and they all laughed again.

'But planes crash,' Sally told her father.

'So do cars . . . but we ride in them every day.'

'But it's more dangerous up in the sky,' Sally argued.

'Not true,' Douglas said. 'You're a lot better off up there.'

'Douglas is right,' Uncle Jack said. 'Planes are more safe than cars.'

'Just as long as I don't have to try it,' Mom said. 'I'll leave the flying to the more adventurous members of the family.'

'Louise . . .' Daddy said, 'I wish you wouldn't talk that way in front of Sally. How will she ever learn to be adventurous?'

'Little girls don't need to be adventurous,' Mom said.

'But I want to be adventurous,' Sally told her.

'Fat chance!' Douglas said. 'You're scared of your own shadow.'

'I am not!'

'So how come you won't go down to the basement by yourself?'

'That's different,' Sally said. 'That has nothing to do with my shadow.'

'That's enough, children!' Mom said.

Aunt Bette and Uncle Jack looked at each other.

Sally turned to her father. 'Will you come for my birthday?'

'I'll try.'

'You have to promise!'

'I'll try my very, very best . . . how's that?'

'Okay . . . I guess.'

Mom took Sally and Douglas to their father's office to have their teeth checked and cleaned before they left for Florida. Ma Fanny didn't have to worry about her teeth because they weren't real. At night she took them out and soaked them in a glass. They clicked when she talked.

Sometimes, when Sally came to her father's office, Miss Kay, Daddy's nurse-secretary, would let her sit at the typewriter, but today she was busy so Sally had to wait with everyone else.

She was glad her father was a dentist. It was fun to have him clean her teeth even though the little brush tickled her gums and made her wiggle around. She'd never had a cavity and Christine said she was really lucky because she had had twenty of them and it didn't tickle to have them filled.

While he cleaned her teeth, Daddy sang to her. He always sang while he worked. He made up the songs as he went along. He could also whistle just like a bird. So Sally gave him the name, Doey-bird. Douglas said it was dumb to name a grown man Doey-bird but Sally's father didn't mind. She liked giving special people special names. She was the one who'd started calling her grandmother Ma Fanny and now everybody called her that. Douglas was just jealous because she hadn't given him a special name too.

If Sally could sing like her father, or even whistle, she wouldn't be in the listener group in music class. It wasn't much fun to mouth the words while practically everyone else got to sing them. Sometimes Sally would forget just to listen and she would sing too. Then Miss Vickers would ask, 'Sally Freedman . . . are you singing out loud?' and Sally would go back to mouthing the words.

After her father finished with her, it was Douglas's turn. Sally hung around until Miss Kay asked, 'Would you like to type for a while?' She gave Sally some yellow paper and adjusted the stool so she could reach the keys. As she typed she heard her father start another song.

Now that he'd had a series of whirlpool treatments, Douglas could use his hands to build things again. He still had to spend a lot of time resting, but instead of lying on his bed reading his favourite magazines, *Popular Science, Popular Mechanics and Model Airplane News* he was making cartoon characters out of eggshells. He had a whole row of them standing on a shelf in his bookcase – Mickey Mouse, Pluto, Donald Duck, Bugs Bunny. Sally liked to watch Douglas blow the insides out of eggshells. And she liked the cakes that Mom and Ma Fanny baked to use up the eggs, too.

As soon as Mom let him go down to his basement workshop again, Douglas abandoned his eggshells in favour of his oscilloscope. He was determined to finish it before they left. It was some kind of machine that let you see electrical waves on a green screen. Sally didn't understand how it worked but everyone else was impressed that Douglas had built it himself.

Mom had a special lamp installed over the work-bench. It was supposed to give Douglas extra vitamin D, like sunshine, until he got to Miami Beach, where they had the real thing. Douglas got a very nice tan on the back of his neck.

During the last week in September Sally invited six school friends home for a farewell lunch. Her mother fixed egg salad sandwiches in different shapes, but Alice Ingram said she was allergic to eggs so Sally's mother made a grilled cheese bun for her. Christine gave Sally a small silver pin with two Scottie dogs on it and said, 'This one's you and this one's me and we're together . . . see . . . best friends for always.' They promised to write at least twice a week.

On 8 October, Sally said goodbye to her classmates and teachers and got her transfer card from the school office. She and Douglas spent the next week at home, in isolation, because Mom didn't want to take any chances that they might come down with something before their trip.

Aunt Bette and Uncle Jack gave up their apartment and arranged to move into Sally's house so her father wouldn't be lonely while the family was away. Sally was glad about that. She didn't like the idea of Daddy living all alone.

It was hardest to say goodbye to him. She sat on his lap with her head on his chest and played with the curly dark hairs on his arm.

'I'm going to finish the basement while you're away,' Daddy told her.

'You are?'

'Yes . . . that's going to be my special project . . . and when you come back we'll have a recreation room.'

'Like Alice Ingram's?'

'I've never seen hers.'

'It's nice,' Sally said. 'Can I have a party in ours?'

'As many as you want.'

'I hope the time goes fast,' Sally said. 'I hope it flies by . . .'

'It will. You'll see. This is going to be an adventure . . .'

'How do you know?' Sally asked.

'Because every new experience is an adventure. Life's full of them. Do you think you can remember that?'

'I'll try . . . but I'll miss you, Doey-bird.'

Daddy hugged her. 'And I'll miss my little gal, Sal.'

'You're so silly!'

'So are you.'

'I wish Mom was silly.'

'She loves you . . . you know that . . . not everybody can be silly.'

'I know . . . but I wish it anyway . . . at least sometimes.'

'You take good care of her, okay?'

'Okay . . .' Sally said. 'Are you ready for your treatment?'

'You know I am.'

'Ready . . . set . . . go . . .' Sally gave him a sliding kiss, three quick hugs and finished with a butterfly kiss on his nose.

'Don't forget to write to me,' Daddy said.

'How could I forget?'

Daddy looked away then. He had tears in his eyes. Sally pretended not to notice. She was having enough trouble holding back her own.

Chapter 4

They left on a Saturday morning, from the railroad station in Newark, on a train called *The Champion*. Douglas was disappointed. He'd wanted to fly. 'Flying is fine for people in a hurry,' Daddy had explained, 'but it's much more expensive and you'll have a good time this way.'

Sally was relieved. She didn't want to fly anywhere but if she told that to her father he might get the wrong idea and think she wasn't adventurous after all. Why wasn't Douglas afraid of anything? That didn't seem fair. Sally felt safe on trains. She was used to them. It bothered her that in this respect she was like her mother.

Daddy came on board, carrying a wicker lunch basket, and helped them get settled in their seats, with Sally and Douglas facing Mom and Ma Fanny. Then he kissed them goodbye for the hundredth time and went back to the platform where he waited with Aunt Bette and Uncle Jack. When the train started Sally waved and blew kisses. And she kept waving until she couldn't see them anymore.

'I'll trade seats with you,' Sally said to Douglas.

'Not now . . . we've only been gone five minutes.'

'You promised you'd share the window seat with me.'

'I'll switch in an hour.'

'Make it half an hour and I won't nudge you.'

'Sit back in your seat, Sally,' Mom said, sounding sharp.

'What for?'

'Because I said so.'

'But I like to sit up . . .'

'Stop that right now,' Mom said, 'or you won't get the window seat at all.'

'Stop what?'

'She can have mine,' Ma Fanny said. 'What do I need with a window seat?'

'No, Ma . . . she can stay right where she is.'

'Yeah,' Douglas muttered.

'Who asked you?' Sally said. She was annoyed at Mom. If Ma Fanny wanted to switch places what did Mom care? Sally turned around and adjusted the white linen napkin clipped to the top of her seat so that her head rested against it. The seats were soft and comfortable, not like the hard ones on the train to New York. These cushions were covered in blue velvet.

Ma Fanny pulled out her knitting. She was the fastest knitter Sally had ever seen. Her needles clicked together as the wool flew off her fingers. Mom knitted more slowly, but her sweaters turned out just as good. Ma Fanny had taught Sally to knit. She could do knit-one-purl-one, and knit-two-purl-two, but her squares always came out with holes in the middle where she'd dropped stitches by mistake.

The train picked up speed and Sally and Douglas watched the scenery whiz by. After a while Douglas took out the latest issue of *Popular Mechanics* and Sally browsed through the two new Nancy Drew books Aunt Bette had given to her as a going-away present. She'd been really surprised to find them inside the pretty package because Aunt Bette didn't approve of Nancy Drews. She thought Sally should be reading the books about the prairie girl.

Sally wrote Christine a postcard.

Dear Christine,
We are on the train now. We've been gone about an hour. That's about all that's new. Write soon.
Love and other indoor sports,
Your very best friend,
Sally Jane Freedman (The First)

Sally didn't know what *Love and other indoor sports* meant but she used to have a baby-sitter named Carolyn who signed all her letters that way. Sally didn't like Carolyn because she was always writing letters. She never had time to play games. One time, when Carolyn left the room for a few minutes, Sally looked at one of her letters and saw how it was signed. When Carolyn came back Sally asked, 'What does *Love and other indoor sports* mean?'

'Have you been reading my letters?' Carolyn asked.

'No.'

'Then how do you know about *Love and other indoor sports*?'

'I saw it, on the bottom of your letter, but I didn't read anything else . . . I promise . . .'

'I hope you're telling the truth,' Carolyn said,

'because you know what happens to nosy little girls, don't you?'

'No . . . what?'

'Nothing very good!'

'Can't you just tell me what *Love and other indoor sports* means?'

Carolyn laughed. 'Some day you'll find out.'

So far she hadn't. But Christine wouldn't know that Sally didn't know.

They ate lunch in their seats. The wicker basket was filled with roast chicken sandwiches, chocolate chip cookies and fresh fruit. When they'd finished, Ma Fanny offered some of the extras to the soldiers sitting behind them.

After lunch Mom and Ma Fanny dozed off and Sally and Douglas walked to the club car. It was fixed up like Alice Ingram's recreation room, with a bar, sofas, and tables and chairs. Douglas bought two Cokes and he and Sally sat at a card table and played a few hands of Go Fish. Douglas won every time.

'Are you glad we're going to Florida?' Sally asked.

'I don't know yet.'

'Same here.'

Douglas reminded Sally of a grasshopper. His legs were growing very long and the shape of his face was long too, and thin, with big brown eyes. He had very nice hair, blond and wavy, the kind Sally would have liked because then Mom wouldn't have to set hers in rag curlers each night.

'Did you know when I first got my kidney infection it burned when I pissed?'

43

'It did?' Douglas was always trying to shock her with bad words.

'Yeah . . . something awful . . . I wanted to climb the walls.'

'You said funny things when you had your fever,' Sally told him.

'Like what, for instance?'

'Oh, I don't remember exactly . . . a lot of mumbo-jumbo stuff . . .'

'No kidding?'

'Honest.'

'Could you make anything out?' Douglas asked.

'No . . . I didn't get to listen that much . . . I was at school all day and then they wouldn't let me in your room most of the time . . .' Sally took a sip of her Coke and promptly got the hiccups.

'You shouldn't drink that stuff.'

'But I like it.'

'Yeah . . . but you get the hiccups every single time.'

'They'll go away.'

'I thought I was going to die,' Douglas said. 'And I didn't even care . . . that's how bad I felt.'

'I thought so too . . . for a little while.'

'No kidding?'

'Really.'

'Were you sorry?'

'Well, naturally . . . who'd want to be an only child?'

'I figured you'd inherit my bicycle.'

'Why would I even want your bicycle?'

'It's newer than yours . . . and bigger . . .'

'So . . . I wouldn't want you to die just because of that . . . don't you think I have any feelings?' She hiccupped loudly and the bartender started to laugh.

When they got back to their seats Mom was still dozing and Ma Fanny was reading *The Forward*, her Yiddish newspaper. Across the aisle and two seats ahead of them was a Negro woman with two little boys and a baby girl. The boys had been watching Sally all morning and now she took some cookies out of the basket and crossed the aisle, offering them to the children.

'How nice,' their mother said. 'Say, *thank you*, Kevin and Kenneth.'

'Thank you, Kevin and Kenneth,' they said at the same time, making Sally laugh. She wasn't as interested in them as she was in the baby, who sat on her mother's lap.

'My name's Sally Freedman and I'm going to Miami Beach because my brother, Douglas, who's sitting right over there, has been sick with a kidney infection . . .'

'Oh, that's too bad. I'm Mrs Williamson and this is Kevin and this is Kenneth.' She touched each boy on the head as she said his name. 'We're going to Miami, too. We're going to visit our granny, who's never seen Loreen.' She held up the baby.

'She's so cute,' Sally said. 'How old is she?'

'Eight months.'

'Hi, Loreen . . .' Sally said. The baby smiled at her. 'I think she likes me. Can I hold her?'

'Sure . . . if you sit down. Kevin, come sit by me and we'll let Sally hold Loreen for a while.'

'You'll be sorry,' Kevin said. 'She makes pooeys.'

'So did you when you were a baby,' his mother reminded him.

Sally got comfortable with Loreen on her lap. As soon as she did the baby grabbed a fistful of her hair and tried to get it into her mouth.

'No, no . . .' Sally said, forcing the baby's fist open.

'And she eats hair,' Kevin said. 'That's how dumb she is.'

Loreen laughed and made gurgling noises.

'She's teething,' Mrs Williamson said. 'Here . . . give her this.' She passed a teething ring to Sally. Loreen put it in her mouth and went, 'Ga-ga'.

'That's all she ever says,' Kenneth told Sally.

Sally held Loreen until the baby fell asleep. Then she gave her back to Mrs Williamson and went to her own seat.

'What were you doing over there?' Mom asked.

'Playing with the baby.'

'You shouldn't be bothering them.'

'I wasn't . . . I was helping . . .'

'From now on just stay in your own seat and read a book or something . . . it's almost time for dinner.'

'Okay . . .' Sally said.

They ate in the dining car, and after took a walk to the club car, where they played checkers. Then it was time to get ready for bed. Sally, Mom and Ma Fanny changed into night clothes in the Ladies' Room and when Sally brushed her teeth Mom warned her not to put her mouth on the fountain when she rinsed. 'You could get *trench mouth* that way, God forbid.' Sally was careful.

There were sleeping compartments on *The Champion* but Sally and her family slept right in their seats. The porter gave them each a pillow and a blanket and showed them how to tilt their chairs way back. The lights in the car dimmed and the steady rhythm of the train soon put Sally to sleep.

She half awoke sometime in the middle of the night, vaguely aware that the train had stopped and that Ma Fanny was snoring softly.

In the morning Loreen and her family were gone. 'But they're going to Miami too,' Sally said. 'Mrs Williamson told me.'

'They had to change cars,' Mom said.

'But why?'

'Because they're Negro.'

'So?'

'We're in a different part of the country now, Sally . . . and coloured people don't ride with white people here.'

'That's not fair.'

'Maybe not . . . but that's the way it is.'

Sally was bored without Loreen, and angry that Mom didn't seem to care that the Williamsons had to change cars. The day dragged on and on. Breakfast turned into lunch and lunch turned into supper. Douglas kept pointing out the change in the scenery. They had to be getting close, he said. There were palm trees everywhere. Sally was tired of just sitting.

She wished she could get off the train and run around.

Finally the conductor called, 'Next stop . . . Miami . . . Miami, Florida . . .'

Finally they were there.

Sally stepped off the train, stretched, and yawned loudly. Now her adventure would begin. But what did that mean? Maybe I don't want an adventure, Sally thought. Maybe I'd just rather go home. Her stomach rolled over, and tears came to her eyes. 'I want to go home,' she said, but no one heard. They were too busy trying to find a porter.

Chapter 5

They took a taxi to 1330 Pennsylvania Avenue, a pink stucco, U-shaped building, with a goldfish pool in front. Their apartment was ugly. Ugly and bare and damp. Mom opened the windows while Sally went looking for the bedrooms, but all she could find was a tiny kitchen, a breakfast nook, a bathroom and an alcove.

'I thought you said this place was interesting,' Sally said to her mother.

'And it is,' Mom answered. 'Look at this . . .' Sally followed her into the alcove and watched as Mom opened a door in the wall and pulled down a bed. 'You see . . . it fits right into the wall . . . it's called a Murphy bed . . . isn't that clever . . . and interesting?' But she didn't sound as if she really thought so herself.

'Who sleeps on that?'

'Me and Ma Fanny,' Mom said. 'You and Douglas get the day beds in the living-room.'

'You and Ma Fanny are going to sleep together . . . in the same bed?'

'Why not?' Ma Fanny asked. 'I don't take up much room.'

'But what about when Daddy comes?'

'Oh, well . . . when Daddy comes Ma Fanny will sleep on the bed that's tucked away *under* your day bed. We have plenty of room . . . plenty . . .' Mom brushed some loose hairs away from her forehead.

Sally thought of the four big bedrooms in her house in New Jersey. Of her own room with twin beds so she could have friends sleep overnight. And then she remembered how Christine had said that only millionaires spend the winter in Florida and she felt like laughing, not because it was funny but because if Christine could see this place she'd change her mind pretty quick.

'So what do you think?' Mom asked Ma Fanny.

'With new slipcovers and curtains, a few plants, some knick-knacks, a throw rug here and there, a picture or two on the wall . . . not bad. Maybe not worth what you had to pay under the table, but not bad. It could be worse.'

'We had no choice,' Mom said, her voice breaking. 'Everything's so scarce right now.'

'Don't worry,' Ma Fanny said, touching Mom's arm, 'as soon as my Singer gets here you'll never recognize the place.'

'Where's the telephone?' Douglas asked.

'We ordered one,' Mom said, 'but it takes a long time . . . there's one in the lobby for emergencies though.'

Douglas nodded.

'At home we have two,' Sally said, suddenly angry. Why were they pretending? Why didn't one of them just admit the truth. This place was a dump. Then she added, 'And we have rose-beige carpeting too!'

'Why don't you just shut up?' Douglas said.

'Who's going to make me?'

'Enough!' Mom said. 'It's been a long trip. Let's get ready for bed. We'll all feel better in the morning.'

It was hard to fall asleep even though Sally felt tired. She tried a story inside her head but that didn't work either. She wasn't used to the smells here, to the strange night noises, to the day bed or having Douglas in the same room, breathing heavily. She missed her father. She wished he was there to tuck her in, although she wasn't under any covers. It was too warm. Just a sheet was more than enough. She wished Daddy was there to give her a treatment.

Two days later Sally got ready for school. She wore her red loafers, her Gibson Girl skirt and blouse and the pin Christine had given to her. Mom braided her hair, then pinned it on top of her head in a coronet because it was too warm to let it hang loose. Ma Fanny kissed her cheek and said, 'Such a shana maidelah.' Sally understood Ma Fanny's Yiddish expressions well enough. Shana maidelah meant pretty girl.

Outside, Sally stopped for a look at the goldfish pool, then she and her mother walked up the street, past yellow and blue and other pink stucco apartment houses.

'One of the reasons we wanted this apartment so badly is that it's very close to school,' Mom said. 'Just one block up and two blocks over . . .' At the corner they crossed the street. 'That's where Douglas will go,' Mom said, pointing to Miami Beach Junior-Senior High.

'When will he start?' Sally asked.

'Tomorrow, I think. First I want Dr Spear to give him a good going-over.'

'Who's Dr Spear?'

'He's going to be our doctor here . . . he was highly recommended . . . he's the best . . .'

'Do I really need this jacket?' Sally asked. 'It's so warm out.'

'I guess not. Give it to me and I'll take it home.'

Sally wriggled out of it.

'You're not nervous, are you?' Mom asked.

'No . . . why should I be nervous?'

'I don't know . . . you didn't eat any breakfast and you've been picking at your cuticles.'

'I'm not used to eating here yet and my cuticles itch . . . that's why I pick at them.'

'I know you'll do just fine,' Mom said, 'so don't be scared.'

'Who's scared?' Sally snapped a big red flower off a bush next to the sidewalk.

'That's a hibiscus,' Mom said.

'It's pretty.' She tucked it behind one ear and twirled around. 'How do I look?'

'Just like Esther Williams,' Mom said.

Sally smiled. Esther Williams was her favourite movie actress. Some day she was going to swim just like her, with her hair in a coronet and a flower behind her ear. Swimming along underwater, always smiling, with beautiful straight white teeth and shiny red lipstick. Esther Williams never got water up her nose or had to spit while she swam, like Sally, who didn't like to get her face wet in the first place. And Esther Williams never splashed either. Not even when she dived off the high board. You'd never know you had to kick to stay afloat from watching Esther Williams. And when she swam in the movies there was always beautiful music in the background and handsome men standing around, waiting. It would be great fun to be Esther Williams!

'This is it,' Mom said. 'Central Beach Elementary School . . .'

'It doesn't look like a school,' Sally said and her stomach growled. 'Oh, be quiet,' she told herself.

'It doesn't look like your school at home,' Mom said.

'That's what I meant.'

'It's Spanish style . . . see the red tile roof . . . and all the archways . . . it's very pretty . . .'

'But it's so big,' Sally said. At home there was just one class for each grade. She knew all the teachers and they knew her. She'd had the same kids in her class since kindergarten. This school was one floor, but it extended for a full block. It was U-shaped too, and made of white stucco. 'And look at all those trailers,' Sally said. 'What do you suppose they're for?'

'They're portable classrooms,' Mom told her. 'The schools down here are crowded.'

'A person could get lost in a school like this.'

'You'll find your way around in no time.'

'And it looks about five hundred years old, too.'

'I doubt that it's *that* old,' Mom said, looking around. 'Now, first of all we've got to find the office.' She stopped a freckle-faced boy. 'Can you tell us where the office is?'

'Yes, Ma'am . . .' he said, 'right around the corridor and second door to your left.'

'Thank you.'

'He called you *Ma'am*,' Sally said.

'Yes, he was very polite.'

'That sounds so funny.'

'I think it sounds nice.'

They found the office and Mom presented Sally's transfer card and school records. The clerk said, 'Well, Sally . . . you'll be in 5B, Miss Swetnick's class . . . and she's one of our nicest fifth grade teachers. I know you'll like her.'

'Thank you,' Sally said, wondering if she should add *Ma'am* but deciding against it.

'Now then . . .' the clerk went on, 'the nurse's office is around the corridor to your right, past the portables and the library, until you come to the art room, then turn left and continue down that corridor until you come to the fourth room on your right . . . it says *Nurse* on the door . . . got that?'

'I think so,' Mom said.

'Why do I have to go to the nurse?' Sally asked.

'It's just a formality,' the clerk told her.

The nurse was fat, with bleached blonde hair in an upsweep. Sally knew it was bleached because the black roots were showing along the part, like when

Mom needed a touch-up. She had two chins and a huge bosom, the kind that went straight across her chest with no space in-between. 'Good morning . . .' she sang, taking the folder from Mom. 'And who do we have here?' She looked inside the folder. 'Sally Freedman?' she asked, as if she were guessing.

'Yes,' Sally said.

'Just get in from New York?'

'New Jersey . . .' How did she know?

'Okay, Sally . . . your mother can wait right here while you come with me . . .' They went into another room. It smelled like alcohol. There were small cots lined up against the wall, with white curtains between them. In the corner was a doctor's scale and next to it, a glass cabinet filled with bandages, bottles and instruments. Sally hoped she wasn't going to get a shot.

'Shoes off, Sally . . . and step on the scale,' the nurse said. As she weighed her she added, 'Don't eat much, do you?'

'Enough,' Sally answered.

'Not very tall either.' The nurse adjusted the marker so that it just touched the top of Sally's head.

'I'm still growing,' Sally said.

'Let's hope so.'

After that the nurse handed Sally a piece of cardboard. 'Cover your left eye, look at the chart on the wall and tell me which way the E is pointing . . . up, down, left or right . . .'

'Don't you have the alphabet here? At home we have charts with all the letters . . .'

'Up, down, left or right . . . if you don't know your left from your right just point . . .'

'I know my left from my right,' Sally said and she began to read the chart. 'Up . . . left . . . right . . . up . . . down . . .'

When both her eyes had been tested and the nurse was satisfied that Sally could see, she said, 'Now have a seat and unbraid your hair.'

'But my mother just fixed it for me . . .'

'And it looks very pretty . . . but I have to check your head before you can be admitted to class, so the sooner you take down those braids the sooner you can get going . . .'

Sally reached up and unpinned her coronet. Then she took the rubber bands off the ends of her braids and unwound them.

The nurse started picking through Sally's hair, messing it up. Sally hoped Mom had a hair brush in her purse. 'Oh, oh . . .' the nurse said, clicking her tongue against the roof of her mouth. 'You've got them.'

'Got what?'

'Nits.'

'In my hair?'

'Where else?'

'What are they?'

'Lice eggs . . . I can't admit you to school with them . . . you'll spread them everywhere . . .'

'But how could I have them? My hair's very clean . . . my mother washed it last night and gave me a vinegar rinse besides . . .'

'No matter . . . shampooing can't get them out . . . you need something much stronger . . . they're nasty little critters. Put your shoes back on while I tell your mother what to do.' She walked out of the room.

Sally jumped into her loafers and listened at the doorway.

'I've never heard anything so outrageous!' Mom said. 'I've always kept my children immaculate. Anyone with eyes can see that. Why, just last night I shampooed her hair . . .'

'Look, Mrs Freedman . . . don't take this personally . . . you've been travelling . . . you're in another part of the country . . . she could have picked them up anywhere . . . it's very common . . . that's why we check the new children so carefully . . . she's not alone . . .'

Mom shook her head. 'You don't understand.'

'Take her home and use the treatment,' the nurse said, 'and in a few days I'll be happy to check her again.'

When Sally heard the word *treatment* her throat tightened and tears came to her eyes.

'I hate it here!' Sally and Mom were walking home from school. 'I hate the nurse and the school and Miami Beach!' She bit her lip to keep from crying.

Mom said, 'Listen, honey . . . that nurse is crazy . . . she doesn't know what she's talking about. You don't have nits. And we'll never tell anyone about it, okay?'

'Then I don't need her treatment after all?' Sally asked brightening.

'Oh, I suppose it can't hurt to go along with her . . . otherwise she might not let you into school . . . but between you and me, there's nothing wrong . . . absolutely nothing . . .'

When they got home Sally went into the bathroom and carefully examined her hair in the mirror. She didn't see anything unusual. She came out and found her mother, Douglas and Ma Fanny talking quietly in the kitchen. They stopped when they saw her.

'Well . . .' Mom said, 'I think I'll go down to the drugstore . . . I'll be back as fast as I can.'

As soon as she'd left Douglas said, 'I hear you got the cooties.'

'I do not have cooties. Mom said there's nothing wrong . . . that nurse is crazy . . . besides, she didn't say *cooties*, she said *nits*.'

'What do you think cooties are?'

'Cooties are make-believe . . . there's really no such thing.'

Douglas started laughing. 'Baloney . . . they're lice . . . little bugs that fly around in your hair . . .' He rubbed his thumb and second finger together.

'You're lying,' Sally said.

'Cootie . . . cootie . . . cootie . . .'

'Ma Fanny,' Sally cried, 'did you hear what he said?'

'Dougie . . . be a good boy,' Ma Fanny said. 'Don't tease Sally.'

'Oh, it was just a joke,' Douglas said. 'Can't she even take a joke?'

'Some joke!' Sally ran across the room and shook her hair at Douglas. 'Have a cootie . . .' she said. 'Have two or three or four . . .'

Douglas ran to the bathroom and locked himself in.

Ma Fanny called, 'Cooties . . . schmooties . . . stop it right now . . .'

Dear Doey-bird,
I miss you very much. Miami Beach is not as great as the ads say. I have a lot to tell you. The nurse wouldn't let me into school because she says I have nits. Do you know what they are? Douglas says they're cooties but I don't believe him. I have this special ointment on my hair now. It's blue and pretty disgusting. I hope it doesn't make my hair fall out. I'm trying to think of this as an adventure, like you said, but so far, it doesn't seem like one because everything is going wrong. Don't feel too bad that I hate it here and want to come home. After all, it's not your fault.
Your loving daughter,
Sally F.

Chapter 6

Two days later Sally went back to school. This time the nurse didn't find anything wrong with her hair and she was admitted to Miss Swetnick's fifth grade class.

The desks were lined up in rows and attached to the floor. Each one had an ink well in the corner. At home they'd had light-coloured wooden desks that moved around and chairs that came in different sizes. And sometimes they'd push their desks together to make tables or else sit two-by-two. Sally knew now that she'd been right about Central Beach Elementary School in the first place. It *was* about five hundred years old.

But Miss Swetnick wasn't. She was young and pretty with red-framed eyeglasses shaped like hearts. She had long black hair tied back with a ribbon and a lot of the girls in the class wore theirs the same way. A few had long braids like Margaret O'Brien, the movie star, but nobody else had a coronet. Another thing Sally noticed right off was their shoes. They all wore sandals – white or gold – and no socks. Sally looked down at her red loafers and thick white socks, which were so popular in New Jersey, and felt foolish.

'Could I please be excused?' Sally asked Miss Swetnick.

Miss Swetnick smiled. Her front tooth was

chipped at an angle. Sally liked the way it looked and wondered if her father could fix her front tooth the same way. 'Already?' Miss Swetnick said. 'You just got here.'

'I know . . . but it's important . . .' Sally shifted her weight from one foot to the other so Miss Swetnick would think it was a real emergency.

'Well . . . I suppose it's all right. But from now on you'll have to go with the rest of the class.'

'I'll remember that,' Sally said.

'The Girls' Room is down the corridor and on your right. Would you like someone from the class to show you the way?'

'No . . . I can find it myself.'

'Hurry back now . . .'

'I will.'

Sally unpinned her coronet on the way to the Girls' Room and put the bobby pins in her dress pocket. Her hair hung below her shoulders in braids. She felt better already. She found the Girls' Room but couldn't believe that there were no doors, not on the outside and not on the inside either. The toilets were separated into stalls but not one of them had a door for privacy. Sally made up her mind never to use the bathroom at school, no matter what. She took off her shoes and socks, then stepped back into her loafers, barefoot. She rolled her socks up in a ball and tried to stuff them into her pocket but they wouldn't go. She had to get rid of them somehow, and fast, so she tossed them into the trash basket, hoping that her mother would never find out. It was a terrible sin to throw away clothing when everyone knew the poor children in Europe were going half-naked. God could punish a person for throwing perfectly good socks away. She hoped he'd understand just this one time.

If Miss Swetnick noticed that Sally had changed her hair or removed her socks, she didn't say. 'We're doing a project on ancient Egypt . . . we're working in committees . . . do you like to draw?' she asked Sally.

'Yes . . . a lot.'

'Good.' Miss Swetnick led her to a group working on the floor, painting a mural. 'Boys and girls . . . this is Sally Freedman. She's from New Jersey and she's going to be in our class. So let's make her feel welcome.'

They looked up at Sally and began to sing.

'We welcome you to Central Beach
We're mighty glad you're here
We'll send the air reverberating
With a mighty cheer
We'll sing you in
We'll sing you out
To you we'll give a mighty shout
Hail, hail, the gang's all here
And you're welcome to Central Bee . . . eeach!'

A boy held a paint brush out to Sally. 'You can put in the woman carrying the jug of water . . . right here . . .' He tapped the paper. 'And make it good . . .'

As she began to sketch, a chubby girl leaned over and put her face so close that Sally could smell her breath. 'I don't like you,' she whispered. 'Get it?'

'I don't like you either,' Sally whispered back because what else could she say to a person who started out that way?

They had Bathroom before lunch and Sally had to go but she wasn't about to use those toilets without doors, although the others did, as if it didn't matter that everyone could see and hear what they were doing. She found out that the girl who didn't like her was Harriet Goodman. Barbara Ash, another girl in the class told her. She also said that Harriet Goodman could play *Peg O' My Heart* on the piano. 'She thinks she's really great because she lives here all year round,' Barbara said. 'She doesn't like winter people.'

'Oh . . . where do you come from?' Sally asked.

'St Louis originally . . . but I live here all the time now . . . only I'm not a snob like Harriet. You want to come to lunch with me?'

'Sure,' Sally said. Barbara had straight blonde hair cut like a Dutch boy's with long bangs. Her skin was suntanned and she had eyes like a dog's, sad but friendly.

Sally had never been in a school cafeteria. In New Jersey she went home for lunch every day. 'Is the food any good?' she asked Barbara, looking around. It was hot and noisy.

Barbara stuck out her tongue and pointed her thumbs down. 'But you're lucky . . . today's spaghetti . . . it could have been meat loaf and that really rots.'

'I don't like spaghetti,' Sally said. 'Can I get something else?'

'Are you kidding? You take what they give you . . . just tell the woman behind the counter you want a small portion . . . and watch for Mrs Walker . . . she's our table monitor this month.'

'A small portion, please,' Sally said, when it was her turn, but the woman behind the counter dumped a load on her plate anyway. Sally picked up a milk carton and followed Barbara to their table.

As soon as they sat down Mrs Walker drawled, 'What's your name, dearie?'

'Sally Freedman.'

'I have certain rules at my table, Sally . . . for one thing, we never wash our food down with our milk. We take small sips after every two mouthfuls. That aids our digestion. And we always clean our plates because so many children are starving in Europe. We have to show we care by not wasting our food. And, of course, we never talk with food in our mouths. Do you have any questions?'

'No,' Sally said.

'No, what, dearie?'

'No . . .' Barbara gave her a kick under the table and mouthed the right word to her. 'No, *Ma'am* . . .' Sally said, feeling stupid.

'That's better. Now you may begin . . .'

★

Sally ran all the way home from school. She had to go to the bathroom in the worst way. She raced up the stairs and past Mom and Ma Fanny, who were waiting at the apartment door, but by then it was too late. Her legs were already wet and as she sat down on the toilet she began to cry. She had never been so ashamed! Maybe God was punishing her for throwing her socks in the trash basket.

'What's wrong?' Mom asked, banging on the bathroom door. 'Are you sick? Sally, let me in.'

Sally flushed the toilet and opened the door. 'I'm never going back!' she cried. '*Never!* There are no doors on the toilets . . . they made me eat a whole plate of spaghetti and I had to sip warm milk after every two bites . . . a girl named Harriet Goodman hates me . . . I wore my hair the wrong way . . . I need sandals . . . I . . .'

Ma Fanny put her arms around Sally and held her until she stopped crying. Then she said, 'So that's the bad news, mumeshana . . . now tell us the good news . . .'

'What good news?' Sally asked.

'Something good must have happened . . . you can't go a whole day without one good thing happening . . .'

'Well,' Sally said, sniffing, 'I met a girl named Barbara. She seemed pretty nice.'

Chapter 7

There were two other apartments in their section. The Daniels lived next door. They had one daughter who was a junior in high school. Her name was Beulah but everybody called her Bubbles. She had rheumatic fever and had to go for check-ups and blood tests every week, like Douglas. The Daniels were very religious and from sundown on Friday till sundown on Saturday they wouldn't answer their doorbell, ride in a car, smoke, turn on the radio or even the light switch. Sally worried that their Sabbath candles would burn the house down.

The Daniels had a mezuzah hanging at the side of their door, like most of the families in the house, but every time they went in or out of their apartment they'd kiss their fingers, then touch their mezuzah. Sally had never known such orthodox Jews.

On Friday, after supper, Sally was sitting on the floor cutting out ballet paper dolls when Mrs Daniels came by with a honey cake for them. 'I'm just on my way to synagogue,' she said. Mom whispered, 'Quick, Sally . . . put away the scissors . . .' Sally thought it was silly of Mom to pretend that they observed the Sabbath like the Daniels. Just because Mrs Daniels wouldn't use a pair of scissors after sundown didn't mean that Sally couldn't. But when she questioned her mother Mom said, 'It doesn't look nice . . . what would they think?'

The Rubins lived across the hall. They were winter people, from Brooklyn – a grandmother, a mother and two kids, like Sally's family. Linda was in second grade and Andrea was in sixth. She and Sally played potsy after school. At home they'd called it hopscotch and had used a rubber heel from the shoemaker. Here it had a different name and they used a stone or a bobby pin, but it was still the same game. Andrea was much taller than Sally – she was even taller than Betsy – with short, dark, curly hair and light blue eyes under heavy brows. She had a dimple in her left cheek and braces on her teeth. When she opened her mouth wide Sally could see the rubber bands way in back.

The Rubins had an all-white cat, called Omar, who slept under the covers with Andrea. He was the most beautiful cat Sally had ever seen but Mom said, 'He may be very pretty but cats can be full of worms so watch out . . . no use looking for trouble.'

Ten days after Sally and her family got to Miami Beach, Ma Fanny's sewing machine arrived, along with their bicycles, a trunkful of clothes and several cartons of household items.

Andrea stood outside with Sally and watched as the movers unloaded their things from the van. 'Now we can go bike riding together!' Andrea said.

'Can I, Mom?' Sally asked.

'Not now,' Mom said, 'it's already close to four.'

'Just to Flamingo Park,' Andrea said, ' . . . it's only a few blocks from here . . . my mother lets me go . . .'

'Oh, please, Mom!'

'You're not an experienced bicycle rider, Sally.'

'I'm experienced enough . . . I hardly ever fall off anymore.'

'I'll watch out for her, Mrs Freedman,' Andrea said.

'And you'll bring her back in an hour?'

'Anything you say . . .'

'Well . . . I guess it's all right then . . .'

'Great!' Andrea said. 'I'll be right back . . . my bike is in the storage room.' While she was gone Sally tried out her own bicycle, making circles in the street. Andrea returned, calling, 'Hey, Douglas . . . want to come to the park with us?'

'Uh uh . . .' Douglas said. 'I'm going exploring on my own.' And he jumped on his bicycle and rode off in the opposite direction.

Sally and Andrea rode to the park on streets lined with palm trees, just like their own.

'Did you know the Pittsburgh Pirates come to Miami Beach in the winter?' Andrea asked.

'You mean the baseball team?' Sally said.

'No . . . I mean the bad guys who rob ships!'

'You *do* mean the baseball team, don't you?'

'Of *course* I mean the baseball team!' Andrea coasted down a small hill.

'I didn't know they came to Miami Beach in the winter.'

'That's what I've been *trying* to tell you . . . they practise in Flamingo Park.'

'I've never been to a big league baseball game,' Sally said, avoiding a stone in the road.

'I have . . . I've seen the Pittsburgh Pirates play . . . at Ebbets Field.'

'Where's that?'

'In Brooklyn . . . right near my house . . . we go to Dodger games all the time.'

'The Brooklyn Dodgers?'

'No . . .' Andrea said, clenching her teeth, 'the Jersey City Dodgers!'

'You *do* mean the Brooklyn Dodgers, don't you?'

'Sally . . . will you quit acting dumb!'

'I'm not acting.'

Andrea took Sally on a bicycle tour around Flamingo Park. The grass was darker green than in New Jersey, but coarse, and Sally already knew, from the yard beside their apartment house, that if you walked on it barefoot, it would scratch the bottoms of your feet.

A group of kids were playing kickball in one of the open areas and some teenagers were stretched out on the grass, soaking up the Miami Beach sunshine. And there were many old people. Sally had never seen so many old people in one place. There were women sitting on park benches, knitting and chatting. There were men, reading and playing cards or checkers.

'Let's go down the bike path,' Andrea said. 'Follow me . . .'

It was a narrow path, surrounded by lush shrubbery. Sally saw a tree with a trunk that looked exactly like the outside of a pineapple. It was strange to see everything so green in October. In New Jersey the leaves would be turning fall colours by now.

Sally noticed the man first. He was sitting alone on a bench next to a clump of trees. As they approached he stood up and blocked their path. 'Hello, little girls,' he said. 'Would you like some candy?' He held a small brown bag out to them.

Andrea reached in and helped herself to a handful of rock candy. 'Thanks . . .' she said, as if she were talking to just anybody.

'You want?' he asked Sally.

After years and years of her mother's warnings it was finally happening. A strange man was offering her candy! Sally took a hard look at him so she could describe him to the police. The police would ask for details and she wanted to be ready to help. Of course, if he murdered her, then she wouldn't be able to help the police at all, but if he murdered only Andrea, then Sally would be able to identify him. He looked familiar, somehow. Who was it that he resembled? Sally chewed on her lower lip and cocked her head to one side. With slick, dark hair and a small black moustache . . . he'd look a lot like . . . like Adolf Hitler! He really would. And the longer she studied his face the more she could see the resemblance.

He shook the bag of candy at Sally. 'Go on . . . take . . .'

'No!' Sally said and rode off, almost knocking the man over.

'What's wrong with you?' Andrea said, pedalling hard to catch up with Sally.

'Don't you know better than to take candy from strangers? He could be a kidnapper or a murderer . . . or worse!'

'He's not a stranger . . .' Andrea said. 'He's Mr Zavodsky.'

'You know him?'

'Sure . . . he lives in our building.' Andrea bit down on a piece of rock candy.

'He could still be a murderer,' Sally said.

'So could anybody!'

'That's what I mean.'

Sally couldn't fall asleep. She tossed and turned, trying out different positions. Legs outside the bed sheet, arms at her sides; arms outside the bed sheet, legs inside. One leg out, one arm out; curled in a ball; spreadeagled on her stomach. Nothing worked. I need a story, she thought.

Sally F. Meets Adolf H.

It is during the war and Sally is caught by Hitler in a round-up of Jewish people in Union County, New Jersey. She has secret information from the head of the east coast underground but she refuses to tell. Hitler can't send her to a concentration camp because he is just building one in Bayonne and it won't be ready for a month. He orders the Gestapo to bring her to his private office. *Tell me, you little swine*, Hitler hisses at her. *Tell me what you know or I'll cut off your hair.*

71

Your threats don't scare me, Adolf, Sally says.

Oh no? We'll see about that! Hitler grabs a pair of scissors and Sally's hair falls to the floor in slow motion until there is a great pile at her feet. *Now you will talk!* Hitler screams.

Never! Sally answers and she sticks her tongue out at him.

That makes him still angrier. He lights a match and one by one burns each of Sally's toes. *Talk . . . talk, you pig . . .*

Sally shakes her head. *I'll never tell you anything . . . never!*

So Hitler goes to his desk and gets his knife and he slowly slashes each of her fingers. She watches as her blood drips onto his rug, covering the huge swastika in the middle.

Look what you've done, you little swine, Hitler cries hysterically. *You've ruined my rug!*

Ha ha, Sally says. *Ha ha on you, Adolf . . .* And then she passes out.

When she comes to, Hitler is asleep and snoring, with his head on his desk. Sally crawls out of his office, then dashes down the hall to the secret passageway of the underground. She gives them valuable information leading to the capture of Adolf Hitler and the end of the war.

On Saturday morning Sally and her family walked to the 15th Street beach with the Rubins. Ma Fanny packed a lunch in the wicker basket and Mom and Douglas each carried a folding chair from Burdines.

72

Sally got to take the old army blanket and the bag with the towels, suntan lotion and dry suits.

At Bradley Beach, on the Jersey shore, the waves were very high and the undertow pulled you in if you weren't careful. Sally clung to the rope there. In Miami Beach there was no boardwalk and no rope. But there were miles and miles of soft yellow sand, bordered by palm trees, and the ocean, even though it was still the Atlantic, wasn't the same at all. The water here was warm and clear and blue-green and when it was low tide you could walk way, way out and still you would only get wet up to your knees.

It took a very long time for Mom to lotion Sally and Sally lost patience and began to wiggle around. 'You could get sun poisoning or a third-degree burn, God forbid,' Mom said, 'so stand still . . . you have to be very careful here . . . the sun is different . . . you should wear your hat . . .'

'Not now . . . maybe later,' Sally said.

'This isn't New Jersey, you know . . .'

'Please, Mom . . .'

'All right . . . one hour without your hat, but don't come crying to me if it's already too late.'

'I won't . . . I promise . . .'

When Mom was finished with Sally she called to Douglas. 'You're next . . .'

'I'll do it myself,' Douglas said, reaching for the lotion.

'You can't get your back . . . you want to wind up in the hospital, God forbid?'

'Dammit! I'm not a baby,' Douglas said, 'so stop treating me like one.'

'Don't you ever let me hear you use that language again!' Mom turned to Ma Fanny. 'He's so stubborn lately,' she said, as if Douglas weren't right there, listening. 'How am I going to manage such a stubborn boy all by myself? He needs his father . . . sometimes I wonder why we ever came here . . .'

'Don't get yourself worked up, Louise,' Ma Fanny said. 'Everything will be all right . . . give it a little time.' She looked across the blanket at Douglas. 'Come, Dougie . . . let me do your back.'

He let Ma Fanny help him without another word.

The Rubins spread their beach blanket next to Sally's, and after Andrea was fully lotioned she and Sally went off together, with Linda running behind them.

Andrea turned perfect cartwheels up and down the beach. Sally tried her best to copy them but she couldn't get both legs up for anything. 'Didn't you ever take acrobatics?' Andrea asked.

'No . . . did you?' Sally knew the answer before Andrea told her.

'I've taken acrobatics since I was seven and ballet since I was eight.'

'I take ballet at home too. I'm in Junior Advanced . . . that is, I would be if I was still in New Jersey.'

'Can you do a backbend?' Andrea asked.

'I don't know . . . I've never tried.'

'Watch this . . .' Andrea bent over backwards and

when her hands touched the sand she flipped up her legs, stayed like that for a second, then stood up and started all over again.

'You're really good,' Sally said.

'I know . . . I'll teach you, if you want . . .'

'Okay . . .'

Andrea put her hands around Sally's waist. 'Now bend over backwards . . . go on . . . I'm holding you . . . don't worry . . . just touch the sand with your hands . . .'

'I'm trying,' Sally said.

'But you're not doing it . . . you're hardly bending at all.'

'I don't think my body goes that way.'

'You have to tell it to . . . you have to send a little message to your brain . . .'

'I'm trying . . . but my brain's not listening.'

'Hi, Sally . . . what are you doing?'

Sally straightened up. It was Barbara. 'Oh, hi, Barbara . . . I'm learning to do a backbend. Andrea's teaching me. Andrea, this is Barbara . . . she's in my class at school.'

'Hi,' Barbara said.

'Hello,' Andrea answered.

'Andrea lives across the hall from me,' Sally said.

'I'm in *sixth* grade,' Andrea told Barbara.

'You look older,' Barbara said.

'I am.'

'Oh, you stayed back?' Barbara asked.

'No! I'm older than you, is what I meant. I'm almost twelve.'

'Oh, I get it,' Barbara said. 'Well, I've got to go now . . . I have to be home by noon. Bye, Sally . . . see you Monday.'

'Bye . . .'

'Eeuuww . . . how can you stand her?' Andrea said, when Barbara was out of earshot. 'She's so . . . so . . . stupid!'

'Not usually,' Sally answered. 'Usually she's very nice. So . . . you want me to try another backbend?'

'No . . . let's get wet instead.'

They ran down to the ocean's edge. 'Can you swim?' Andrea asked.

'Some,' Sally told her. 'Can you?'

Andrea sat in the wet sand and held her knees to her chest. 'I could if I wanted to but I feel better with my feet on the bottom . . . do you know what I mean?'

Sally tried not to smile. She picked up a handful of wet sand and let it ooze through her fingers. 'I can float on my back. I might be able to teach you.'

'Maybe,' Andrea said, shielding her eyes from the sun. 'Look . . . there's the Goodyear Blimp.'

Sally looked up and saw a big grey bubble floating over the ocean, in the sky. The word GOODYEAR was printed on its side.

Linda ran in front of them then, splashing. 'Ha ha . . .' she called, 'got you wet . . . got you wet . . .'

'Go back to Mommy,' Andrea yelled. 'You know you're not allowed in by yourself.'

'*Tinsel Teeth*,' Linda called, '*Railroad Tracks* . . .'

Andrea picked up a handful of sand and tossed it at Linda. 'Get out of here, you little brat!'

Linda ran toward her mother.

'She's getting so spoiled,' Andrea said. 'I can't stand it. Just because she almost died my mother lets her get away with murder . . . and my grandmother's just as bad . . .'

'I didn't know she almost died,' Sally said.

'Last April . . . she had polio . . .'

'Really? You can't tell . . .'

'I know it . . . she's fine now . . . but that's why we're here . . . they don't want her to get sick again . . .'

'Sound's like us,' Sally said, 'except if I ever called Douglas *Tinsel Teeth* or *Railroad Tracks* I'd really get it . . . my father's a dentist!'

'Mine manufactures bras and girdles.'

'Really?'

'Uh huh . . . he's coming down for Thanksgiving . . . want me to ask him to bring you some bras?'

'I don't wear them yet.'

'I noticed . . . but some day you might.'

'I hope so.'

'I don't miss my father at all . . . do you miss yours?'

'Yes, a lot. He's coming down for Thanksgiving too. I can't wait!'

'My father's very busy . . . I hardly ever see him at home . . .'

'My father's busy too but he always has time for me.'

Chapter 8

Dear Doey-bird,
Miami Beach is full of bugs. You never saw so many
bugs. Big ones, little ones, they are everywhere. I
especially hate water bugs. They give me the creeps.
Also, outside you can see salamanders. They are
lizards that change colours. Or did you already know
that? Douglas wants to keep one for a pet but Mom
won't let him. But here is the biggest news yet. We
had to set mouse traps in the kitchen! Ma Fanny
discovered the mice. That is, she heard them running
around at night. She says in Miami Beach it doesn't
mean you don't keep a clean kitchen. Just about
everybody has them, and bugs too. Mom bought three
mouse traps. We caught our first mouse this morning.
Douglas got elected mouse remover and had to throw
him in the garbage. He picked him up by the tail!
  I like the beach here very much except Mom makes
me change out of my wet suit before lunch. She says
Douglas got his kidney infection from sitting around in
wet clothes. I told her, Mom, this is the beach . . .
you're supposed to get wet. She didn't think that was
very funny. I wouldn't even mind changing if she'd
just let me go to the bathhouse to do it. But she says
I might pick up something very bad there. I asked her
What? but she says it's better if I don't know. Andrea's
mother told her the same thing. We think it's some
kind of disease.

Do you know of a special disease you can get from bathhouses? If so, write and tell me. If not, write and tell Mom so I don't have to change out in the open any more. Mom says no one can see anything because she holds up a towel to cover my front and Ma Fanny holds one up to cover my back, making a little closet for me. I keep my eyes shut the whole time because if anyone is looking I don't want to know. Douglas doesn't have to change because he never gets wet!

Do you know about Man O'Wars? They are bluish bubbles that sometimes float around in the ocean. When there are a lot of them the lifeguards won't let you go in the water. They're pretty dangerous. They can sting you. Douglas poked one that had washed up on the beach, with a stick, and Mom got sooo mad. She said Douglas chases trouble. But the Man O'War was already dead. Douglas was just interested in its insides.

In school we are studying the history and geography of Florida. Can't wait to see you.
Your loving daughter,
Sally F.

Sally folded her letter, put it in an envelope, and sealed it. Then she took another piece of paper from her box of Bambi stationery and wrote:

Dear Mr Zavodsky,
You don't know me or who I am and you'll never find out, not if you guess for twenty years. But I think I know who you are. I think you are a person

*people hate. I think you are a person who is wicked
and evil. I think you are worse than a regular
murderer or kidnapper. I think you are a person
with the initials A.H.*

She folded that letter and put it in her keepsake box,
under the day bed. Tomorrow she might mail it.

Sally got a special letter from her father. It was
written in red ink on a yellow balloon. She had to
blow it up before she could read it.

*Dear Sally,
How's my gal? Thought you might like to get a
different kind of letter so here it is. I saw Christine
yesterday. She asked for your address so she can
write to you. I miss you too! Soon it will be
Thanksgiving and I'll be there for my treatment.
Stay well. Take good care of Mom for me.
Love and kisses,
Doey*

*Dear Doey-bird,
Hi! I loved your balloon letter. I'm saving it in my
keepsake box, along with my marble collection,
some shells from the beach and a very pretty flower
I picked up on my way home from school. I'm
glad the balloon didn't pop when I blew it up. You
didn't answer my question about the bathhouse
disease. Please tell me what you know. It's very
important! I have a new friend. Her name is Shelby*

and she lives at the corner. Don't get her mixed up with Andrea, who lives across the hall. Andrea is in sixth grade and has a cat called Omar. Don't get her mixed up with Barbara either. Barbara is my friend from my class. Shelby is in fifth grade too but not in my section. Her classroom is in a portable. She lives with her grandmother and has a neat game called Jolly Roger. I sure wish I had it too. We met because she goes home for lunch every day, like me. We both got special permission because we are allergic to the food at school. Well, not really allergic, but that's what we said. Finally we decided to walk back and forth together. When I'm done eating lunch I call for her and if there's time we play some Jolly Roger before heading back to school. Shelby's mother and father are getting a divorce. That's how come she's here. They're having a big fight over who gets her and she's not supposed to know about it. She hates them both. I don't blame her.

Next week is Halloween. There's going to be a parade in Flamingo Park at night. A flamingo is a tall pink bird with skinny legs. Or did you already know that? Anyway, Andrea is going to dress up like one. She's tall enough!

Mom came up with an idea for my costume. I'm going to be a peanut girl. She is sewing peanuts all over my old green dress. And she's making me a crown out of cardboard that will have peanuts glued to it. Even my socks have peanuts on them. Mom has two infected fingers from pushing the sewing needle through the peanuts, but don't worry. Ma

Fanny knew just what to do and Mom is soaking her fingers right now.

I am still blotchy red from the sun, but Douglas is already very tanned. The pimples on his chin are clearing up. Mom says the Miami Beach sunshine is really some medicine. But she is worried that Douglas isn't making new friends here. At home he didn't have that many either so I think she should just leave him alone. He likes to explore by himself. He is also busy inventing a coconut catcher. He wants to get coconuts off the trees when they are just ripe enough, but before they get rotten. He loves to eat them and drink their milk. I tried one the other day but yuck . . . I spat the whole thing out. Does that mean I'm not adventurous? I hope not! When you take the shell off a coconut it looks like it has a face. Or did you already know that?

I miss you very, very, very much! I can't wait until Thanksgiving either. I will give you such a treatment then. Say hello to Aunt Bette and Uncle Jack and Miss Kay and anyone else you think might miss me.

Your loving daughter,
Sally F.
P.S. Jolly Roger is the best game I've ever played!

Chapter 9

On Sunday mornings, at exactly ten o'clock, Sally, Douglas and Mom went down to the lobby to wait for Daddy's phone call. The phone was too high on the wall for Sally to reach so she stood on a chair. This was her Sunday to answer.

'Doey-bird!' Sally shouted, when the phone rang and she heard her father's voice at last.

Douglas hissed, 'Will you shut up with that dumb name before everybody hears it.'

Sally motioned for Douglas to shut up himself.

'How's my little gal?' Daddy asked.

'Fine . . . but I miss you.'

'I miss you too.'

'Last night we went to the movies and nobody wanted to sit next to me because they say I ask too many questions . . . but if you don't ask questions then you'll never learn anything . . . isn't that right? And did you hear about Halloween? There was this huge thunderstorm in the middle of the parade and all the lights in the park went out and you should have heard all the screaming but I wasn't scared because it was an adventure . . .'

Douglas muttered under his breath, 'Not much . . .'

'Anyway, Doey . . . I wasn't *that* scared . . . and we got home okay . . . just all my peanuts got soggy and we had to throw away my whole costume.' She paused for a breath. 'And in school the music teacher lets me sing . . . she even likes the way I sing . . .'

Douglas mumbled, 'Ha ha . . .'

'Well, she does . . . not like dumb old Miss Vickers who always made me be in the listener group . . .'

Douglas tried to grab the phone away but Sally held on and told her father, 'Douglas is trying to take the phone from me and I don't know why because he never even has anything to say and I have a lot to say and listen, Doey . . . the goldfish in the pool in our courtyard are *so* big . . . you never saw goldfish *so* big in your life and . . .'

Douglas grabbed again. 'Okay, Douglas! Just one more thing, Doey . . . my friend Andrea has a cat . . . I wrote you about him . . . he's so soft and he purrs when you pet him and I know he hasn't got any worms. So will you please tell Mom it's okay for me to play with him? And what about the bathhouse disease? Oh . . . well, don't forget . . . okay, I'll listen to her . . . yes, I promise . . . Douglas is practically *breaking* my arm . . . I love you too. Here, Douglas,' Sally said, shoving the phone at him. 'I hope you have something important to say this time.'

'Hi, Dad . . .' Douglas said. 'I'm okay . . . they're okay . . . it's okay . . . yeah, I feel fine . . . yeah, I'm trying . . . yeah, I know . . . yeah . . . well, here's Mom . . .' He passed the phone to his mother.

'Oh, Arnold . . .' Mom said, sniffling. Douglas went outside. Sally stayed where she was, hoping to hear the rest of the conversation but Mom waved her away, saying, 'Go play . . .'

'Do I have to?'

'Yes . . . hurry up . . . outside . . .'

'Oh, all right!' Sally went outside, in time to catch Douglas, walking his bicycle from the storage room to the street. 'Hey, Douglas, wait up . . .' she called. 'I'll ride with you.'

'No, thanks . . .'

'Where are you going, anyway?'

'Exploring.'

'Exploring where?'

'All over,' he said and pedalled away.

Sally sat on the edge of the goldfish pool. It was so quiet this morning. Where was everybody? Probably still sleeping. It was going to be hot today, a real sizzler, as Ma Fanny would say. Later they'd go to the beach. Sally watched a salamander work its way up a bush, changing its colour to blend in with its surroundings. Lucky salamander! It would be nice to become invisible like that, sometimes. If she had been able to blend right into the sofa in the lobby she could have listened to Mom talking to Daddy. And what did Mom have to say to him that was so private anyhow? Yes, it would be very nice to be invisible whenever you wanted.

Sally looked into the goldfish pond. I am invisible . . . I can see you, fish, but you can't see me . . . She tossed a pebble at her own reflection and watched as the ripples distorted her face. Invisible . . . invisible, she thought, closing her eyes.

When she opened them another reflection appeared in the pool, next to hers. She turned around and caught her breath. *Mr Zavodsky!* He was standing very close to her. Close enough to reach out and touch her. Close enough to push her into the gold-fish pool.

'Hello, little girl . . . you want some candy?'

'No!' Sally jumped up and tore off into the house. She rushed up the stairs and burst into her apartment. 'Do you know Mr Zavodsky?' she asked Mom.

Mom was sitting in the stuffed chair in the corner, one hand covering her eyes. 'I know of him . . . why?' She sniffled and took her hand away from her face.

'I don't like him!' Sally said.

'Why . . . did he do something to you?' Mom looked concerned.

'He offered me candy.'

'I hope you didn't take any.' Mom wiped her nose with a Kleenex.

'I didn't . . . but one time Andrea did.'

'She should know better.'

'That's what I told her.'

'Stay away from him,' Mom said, ' . . . and where's your brother?'

'Out on his bike . . . exploring . . .'

'Oh, God . . . what am I going to do?' Mom asked, her voice breaking.

'About what?' Sally asked.

But Mom didn't answer. She ran to the bathroom.

On Thursdays schools were closed because of a teachers' meeting. Sally went down to the lobby to wait for Shelby, who was coming over for lunch. She wondered if Mr Zavodsky would be there, with his bag of candy. If he was, she'd have to warn Shelby. She'd tell her he was a dangerous stranger, but no more.

Mr Zavodsky wasn't in the lobby but Bubbles Daniels from next door was, talking on the pay phone. Sally sat down on the sofa. Bubbles had pretty hair, the colour of carrots. She was almost seventeen. Sally wound her braid around her finger, thinking, Bubbles is older than Tante Rose when she had Lila.

Bubbles put her hand over the mouthpiece and spoke to Sally. 'I'll just be another minute.'

'That's okay,' Sally told her, 'I'm not waiting for the phone.'

'Oh . . . then could you possibly go outside?'

'What for?'

'So I can finish my conversation.'

'I don't mind if you finish.'

'I'd like to finish in *private*,' Bubbles said.

'Oh . . . why didn't you say so in the first place?' Sally walked outside. As she did, she heard Bubbles say, 'Will I be glad when we finally get a phone upstairs!'

'Everybody's got secrets these days,' Sally muttered to herself.

Sally met Shelby out front. 'I brought my Jolly Roger game,' Shelby said.

'Good.'

They went into the lobby. Bubbles was still on the phone. 'Just a minute . . .' she said into it, giving

Sally and Shelby a nasty look. When they were on the stairs, Bubbles went back to her conversation. 'The *children* in this house are driving me crazy!'

'She's my next door neighbour,' Sally told Shelby.

'Lucky you!' Shelby said.

Sally opened the door to her apartment and called, 'Shelby's here . . .'

Shelby looked around. 'Your place is so pretty!'

'Thanks . . . you should have seen it before . . .' Sally had to admit that Mom and Ma Fanny had done a nice job. The apartment was bright and cheerful now, with plants and curtains and plaid slip-covers on the day beds. There were pictures of boats and sunsets hanging on the walls and Ma Fanny's collection of family snapshots standing on all the small tables. There were twenty-two photographs in silver frames, four of them showing Tante Rose and Lila at different ages. Sally picked up her favourite. 'This is Lila, my cousin, once removed. She died in a concentration camp.'

'That's too bad.'

'Doesn't she have big eyes?'

'Yes.'

'You can tell she's happy even though she isn't really smiling, can't you?'

'Sure.'

Sally wanted to grow up to look just like Lila. She hoped her eyes would get bigger and her hair heavier, and that you would know she was smiling even when her mouth was closed. And then, when she finally parted her lips – what a surprise – a beautifully chipped front tooth, exactly like Miss Swetnick's.

Sally and Shelby had sour cream and cottage cheese for lunch and for dessert, ladyfingers with grape jelly. After, they played three games of Jolly Roger.

'Would you like to play something else now?' Sally asked.

'Like what?'

'Oh, I don't know . . . we could play Pretend . . .'

'Pretend what?'

'Cowgirl or Detective or War . . . something like that.'

'I wouldn't mind playing Cowgirl,' Shelby said. 'What are the rules?'

'There aren't any . . . I make up the story and we play . . . it's easy . . .'

'I don't know . . . I'm not very good at games without rules.'

'Well . . . if you don't want to . . .'

'What about marbles?' Shelby said, 'I like to shoot marbles.'

'I have a great collection!' Sally said, jumping up. 'Wait till I show you my favourite . . . clear green all over . . .' She pulled her keepsake box out from under the day bed, opened it, and took out a small cloth bag. She emptied it on the floor, in front of Shelby.

'Next time I'll bring my collection over,' Shelby said. 'I've got one that's pure black!'

That night Mom took Sally and Douglas to the movies to see *The Farmer's Daughter*. Even though

Sally loved movies she missed seeing them with her father, because without Daddy there was no one to act out scenes with her after the show. And when she asked questions during the movie, Mom and Douglas just said, *shush . . .*

But there were some things in Miami Beach that were better than in New Jersey. One of them was Herschel's Sweet Shoppe. Mom always took them to Herschel's after the movies. Herschel knew just how to make Sally's sundae. She never had to remind him. One scoop of chocolate ice cream, one scoop of vanilla, lots of fudge sauce, a great pile of whipped cream and just a touch of cherry juice on top, but not the cherry itself. Herschel got it right every time.

Chapter 10

It was Wednesday afternoon and Miss Swetnick was dictating a poem to the class. They would be graded on spelling and handwriting. Sally dipped her stick pen into the inkwell in the corner of her desk. She glanced across the aisle at Barbara. Barbara had the best handwriting in the class. At least Miss Swetnick thought so. She always gave her an E for excellent while Sally never got more than a G for good. She was hoping for an E today. She watched Barbara form her letters and she tried to make hers look the same. Big and round with lots of space between each word. She didn't worry much about spelling because she never got more than one or at the most two words wrong. Not like Peter Hornstein. He sat behind her and got five or six words wrong every week and since you had to write every misspelled word twenty-five times in the back of your book he never caught up and had to stay after school a lot.

When Miss Swetnick had finished dictating they folded their hands on their desks and she walked up and down the aisles grading their papers. Sally dug her nails into her palms. She hoped, she prayed, that today would be the day she'd get an E, but when Miss Swetnick came by she hardly glanced at Sally's paper. She just made a big G in red pencil at the top, smiled, and said, 'Your letters are too big and there's too much space between each word.'

Barbara got another E for excellent.

As soon as Miss Swetnick moved to another aisle Sally felt a tug on her right braid. She whipped around in her seat to tell Peter Hornstein to leave her hair alone once and for all and when she did her braid hit her face.

'Miss Swetnick . . . Miss Swetnick . . .' Sally called, wiping ink off her cheek. 'I've got ink all over me . . .' She held up her hand to show Miss Swetnick.

Barbara leaned across the aisle. 'It's on the back of your dress, too,' she whispered.

'Oh . . . and it's on my dress . . . my mother's going to kill me!'

'How did that happen?' Miss Swetnick asked.

'I don't know,' Sally said.

'Peter . . . did you dip Sally's hair in your inkwell?'

'Yes, Ma'am,' Peter said. 'By accident.'

Sally turned round in her seat. 'You dipped my braid in your ink?'

'It got in the way,' Peter said. 'It's always in the way . . . hanging onto my desk . . . tickling my fingers . . .'

'Peter,' Miss Swetnick said, 'Sally's braids hang straight down her back, not onto your desk. You must have reached out for one of them . . .'

Sally glared at him.

He smiled back.

'Oh, Peter . . .' Miss Swetnick sighed and took off her glasses. 'What am I going to do with you?'

'I don't know, Ma'am,' Peter said.

From the back of the room, where the tallest kids

in the class sat, Harriet Goodman called, 'You should send him to the office, Miss Swetnick.'

'When I want your advice, Harriet, I'll ask for it,' Miss Swetnick said.

'I thought you did . . . you said that you don't know . . .'

'I *know* what I said. Thank you, Harriet!' Miss Swetnick came over to Peter's desk and shook her head. 'You'll have to stay after school again. This time the blackboards get washed, the plants get watered and you'll write *I will not misbehave in class* twenty-five times in your best handwriting.'

'But Miss Swetnick . . .' Peter said, 'I have six spelling words to write. I'll never get done.'

'Maybe you'll remember that before you start fooling around again.'

'Yes, Ma'am.'

'Sally, go and wash off your face.'

'What about my hair and my dress?'

'You can do that at home.'

'Yes, Miss Swetnick.' She still couldn't bring herself to say *Ma'am*.

As they were lining up to go home Harriet Goodman stood behind Sally and said, 'Miss Swetnick will never send Peter to the office because she goes with his brother. Everybody knows that . . . and I still don't like you . . .'

After school Sally went to Barbara's. She lived a few blocks up from Sally in a yellow building with hibiscus bushes out front. Her apartment was on the first floor and had a damp smell. Sally remembered Mom saying that first floor apartments were no good in Florida because of the dampness. There was nobody home.

'My mother works,' Barbara said. 'She gets home at five-thirty.'

'Oh.' Sally didn't know anybody who had a working mother.

'She's a secretary for National Airlines.'

'My father might fly National at Thanksgiving.'

'My mother says they're all the same. Want a glass of milk?'

'If you do.'

'I do if you do.'

'Well, it doesn't matter to me.'

'Okay . . . then I'll have some.'

'Okay . . . me too.'

'Want a fig newton with it?' Barbara asked.

'They're my favourites.'

'Mine too.'

'My sister likes butter cookies best.'

'I didn't know you have a sister.'

'Yes . . . her name's Marla . . . she'll be home later . . . she's in tenth grade.'

'My brother's in ninth . . . but he should only be in eighth . . . he's a genius.'

'My sister's not . . . but she's a majorette . . . she can twirl two batons at once.'

'I can't even twirl one.'

'Me neither . . . but I'm going to learn.'

'Maybe I can too,' Sally suggested.

'Yes, we could learn together.'

'That'd be fun,' Sally said. 'Except I don't have a baton.'

'Maybe you can get one . . .' Barbara said. 'Want to see my room?'

'Sure.'

They grabbed a few more cookies and carried their milk glasses through the small living-room to the bedroom.

'Peter Hornstein likes you,' Barbara said.

'He does?'

'Yes . . . otherwise he wouldn't dip your hair in his inkwell.'

'Really?' This was certainly news to Sally.

'Yes . . . my sister's an expert on that stuff and she told me that if a boy teases you it means he likes you.'

'Well . . . I don't mind,' Sally said. 'I think he's cute . . . don't you?'

'No . . . I think he looks like a chimpanzee.'

'Just because his ears stick out?' Sally asked.

'That and the shape of his mouth.'

'Harriet Goodman says Miss Swetnick goes with Peter's brother . . .'

'She does,' Barbara said. 'Everybody knows . . .'

'I never knew.'

'You do now!' Barbara sat down on a bed. 'This is my side of the room . . . I like my things neat and Marla's a slob so my mother divided the room for us.'

Barbara's bed was covered with a white spread and

on her shelves were rows of miniature dolls and jelly glasses filled with sharpened pencils. Marla's side of the room was a mess, with an unmade bed and clothing all over the floor.

'Where does your mother sleep?' Sally asked.

'In the living-room . . . on the sofa.'

'How about your father . . . when he comes down?'

'My father's dead,' Barbara said, slurping up the last of her milk. She brushed the crumbs off her hands into the waste basket. 'You want to see his picture?'

'Sure.' Sally didn't know what else to say.

Barbara took a silver framed photo from the top of her dresser and handed it to Sally. The picture showed a handsome man in a uniform and across the bottom he had written, *For my darling daughters, Marla and Barbara, Love always, Daddy.* 'He got it in the Pacific,' Barbara said. 'Right in the gut . . .' She punched herself in the stomach. 'They sent us his dog tags.'

'Who?'

'Washington . . . the marines . . . you know . . .'

'Oh.'

'I can show them to you if you want . . . I know where my mother keeps them.'

'Okay.'

Sally followed Barbara into the living-room where she opened a desk drawer and pulled out a velvet jewellery box. She handed it to Sally. 'Go on . . . open it . . .'

Sally raised the lid. Inside was a chain with Barbara's father's dog tags.

'His name was Jacob Ash . . . but my mother and everyone else called him Jack. We moved here after . . . she needed to get away . . . she cried a lot . . . he had big hands . . . when I was little he carried me on his shoulders so I wouldn't get tired . . . at first I hated him for dying but now I understand it wasn't his fault . . .' Barbara closed the box and put it back in the drawer. 'Let's go outside,' she said. 'We can play statues.'

When Sally got home her mother said, 'Sally Freedman . . . what happened to your dress?'

'Nothing much . . . it's just ink,' Sally said.

'How did that happen . . . ink won't come out . . . the dress is ruined . . .'

'It was an accident,' Sally said. 'My braid got into Peter Hornstein's inkwell by mistake and then I shook my head and the ink splattered . . .'

'That's no excuse . . .'

Sally looked around. 'Where's Ma Fanny?'

'At her card game . . . why?'

'Because *she'd* know what to do!'

'I know what to do, too,' Mom said. ' . . . Soak it in seltzer water . . . but that's not the point. You've got to learn to take care of your things . . . I can't afford to replace them . . . money doesn't grow on trees!'

'There are some things that are more important than money,' Sally shouted, 'or clothes!' And sud-

98

denly she started to cry. She ran for the bathroom. When Mom knocked on the door Sally opened it halfway and handed her the soiled dress.

Chapter 11

Sally was stretched out on the floor, drawing. 'How old is Daddy going to be on his birthday?' she asked her mother.

'Forty-two,' Mom said, looking up from her book. 'Why?'

'I want to put it on this card I'm making him,' Sally said, pulling a green crayon from her box of Crayolas. 'How soon do I have to mail it?'

'Tomorrow, to be safe,' Mom said. 'His birthday's the fifteenth.'

'What do you think of my rhyme?' Sally asked. '*Forty-two and I love you!*'

'Original . . .' Douglas said, munching on a piece of coconut. 'Very original.'

Sally made a face at him and thought harder. 'How about this? *Don't be blue just because you're forty-two.*'

'Oh, God . . .' Mom jumped up and ran into the bathroom.

'Smart,' Douglas said to Sally. 'Very smart . . .'

'What'd I do?'

'You had to go and bring up the subject.'

'What subject?'

'Dad's age.'

'So, it's his birthday.'

'Yeah . . . but Uncle Eddie and Uncle Abe were both forty-two when they died . . . did you know that?'

'No,' Sally said. 'That's impossible . . . I remember them . . . they were both old . . .'

'It seemed that way to you because you were only four or something . . .'

'I don't believe you,' Sally said, standing up.

'Why else do you think she's in there crying?' Douglas nodded in the direction of the bathroom.

'Who says she's crying?' It made Sally uncomfortable to think of Mom crying.

Douglas shrugged and headed for the door.

'Where are you going?' Sally asked.

'Out.'

'Can I come?'

'No!' He let the screen slam shut.

Sally wished Ma Fanny were home instead of out walking with Andrea's grandmother. They walked together just about every night, after supper.

Later, when Sally went to bed, she couldn't stop thinking about her father, and then about Barbara. Barbara was the only friend she had with no father. Even though very few of her new friends lived with their fathers, they still had them. But not Barbara. Her father was dead . . . killed in the war. How would it feel to know your father was dead and not coming down for Thanksgiving . . . that you would never see him again . . .

Sally prayed hard. *Please God, let Doey-bird get through this bad year . . . this year of being forty-two . . . we need him, God . . . we love him . . . so don't let him die.* She started to cry quietly, worrying that her father was lonely, that something terrible would

101

happen to him. *Keep him well, God . . . you wouldn't let three brothers die at the same age, would you?* But somewhere in the back of her mind she remembered hearing that bad things always happen in threes. If only she was home in New Jersey now . . . she'd watch her father carefully . . . she'd make sure he got plenty of rest and if he caught cold or something she'd make him go straight to bed and stay there . . . and she'd get him to stop smoking two packs of Camels a day . . .

Finally she drifted off to sleep. She dreamed Miss Kay had died. It was raining and they were all at her funeral – Sally, Douglas, Mom, Aunt Bette, Uncle Jack, Ma Fanny. Miss Kay just lay in her coffin, dressed in her nurse's uniform. She had a kind of smile on her face and was wearing bright red lipstick. But where was Daddy? Why wasn't he there too? Sally called out and sat up.

'Shut up,' Douglas said, 'some people are trying to sleep.'

'I had a bad dream,' Sally told him.

'Well, it's over now so go back to sleep.'

At breakfast the next morning Sally said, 'I dreamed Miss Kay was dead.'

'That means she's going to get married,' Ma Fanny said, pouring the juice.

'It does? But how would *I* know that she's going to get married?'

'When you dream somebody dies it means they're

going to get married,' Ma Fanny said. 'Everybody knows that . . . right, Louise?'

'Yes,' Mom said, 'of course . . .' She was browsing through the morning paper, sipping a cup of tea.

'But suppose the person is already married and you dream that?' Sally said, mashing her shredded wheat.

'That means the person will stay happily married for years and years,' Ma Fanny answered. 'Right, Louise?'

'Right,' Mom said, looking up from the paper. 'And Miss Kay would be very happy to hear about your dream because she'd like to meet a nice man and get married.'

'You think I should write and tell her about it?'

'Oh, you don't have to do that,' Mom said. 'You can wait until the next time you see her.'

'But I won't see her for a very long time.'

'That's okay,' Mom said. 'It'll keep.'

Douglas was reading the back of the cereal box. He never had anything to say in the morning.

'Ma Fanny . . .' Sally said.

'What, sweetie-pie?'

'Do you believe that bad things always happen in threes?'

'Not always . . . but sometimes,' Ma Fanny said.

'How can you tell when it will be like that . . . when something bad will happen three times?'

Now Douglas looked over at Sally, as if to warn her to cut it out.

'You can't tell,' Ma Fanny went on. 'You wait and see . . . then if it happens three times, you know . . .'

'But that doesn't make sense,' Sally said.

'Finish your cereal,' Mom told her, 'or you'll be late for school.'

'It's all superstition anyway,' Douglas said, yawning.

'I'm superstitious?' Ma Fanny asked.

'Yes,' Douglas said. 'You knock on wood and all that stuff.'

'Just to be careful . . . just in case . . .' Ma Fanny said, 'but not because I'm superstitious.'

'You told me once if a bird craps on you it's good luck,' Douglas said.

'Douglas!' Mom sounded shocked, but not angry. 'Watch your language.'

'Sorry . . . if a bird lets out his stuff on you . . .'

'Douglas!' Now she sounded angry.

'Well, how else can you say it?' Douglas asked.

'If a bird *plops* on you,' Sally suggested.

'That's enough!' Mom told them both and Sally and Douglas smiled at each other. He could be such fun when he wanted to. Sally wished he'd want to more often.

'How do you know all those things, Ma Fanny?' Sally asked.

'My mother told me . . . when I was a little girl.'

'Some people respect what their mothers say.' Mom aimed this remark at Douglas.

'Bully for some people,' Douglas answered.

Sally got a letter from Christine.

104

Dear Sally,

*Hi! How are you? I am fine. Alice Ingram showed
the boys her underpants in the cloakroom. They
were light blue with lace around the edges. I always
knew she was a show-off! Miss Vickers put me
into the listener group in music. I guess I am taking
your place. My mother is really mad and is going to
complain to the principal. I already know all the
Thanksgiving songs by heart and I want to sing them,
not just pretend. Our programme is the usual, with
Pilgrims and Indians and stuff. I hope you are
having fun with the other millionaires. You are still
my best friend, but until you come home I am
pretending that Joan is.*

*Love and other indoor sports (what does that mean,
anyway?),*

Chrissy (this is what I now call myself)

After supper all the neighbourhood kids came out
to play hide and seek. It didn't get dark as early here
as in New Jersey and Sally was allowed to stay outside
until eight o'clock on school nights. Mom wouldn't
let Douglas ride his bicycle after supper so he sometimes joined the hide and seek game too. Lately,
Andrea tried to hide with Douglas. Sally didn't like
that and was pleased when Douglas told Andrea,
'Quit following me . . . go and hide with Sally.'

Tonight, Shelby was It. She had to hide her eyes
by the big palm tree and count to 120. Sally and
Andrea ran off to hide behind the row of bushes

near the sidewalk. The bushes grew so high and thick it was easy to stay out of sight.

'Ready or not, here I come . . .' Shelby shouted and went off to search on the other side of the house.

'Should we run in?' Sally asked. 'I think we can make it.'

'Not yet,' Andrea said.

'Hello, little girls . . .'

They turned around. *Mr Zavodsky, again!*

'Shush . . .' Andrea said, putting her finger to her lips. 'We're in the middle of a game.'

He made a hand motion to show he understood and went away.

'I don't like him,' Sally said. 'He's always sneaking up on people.'

'No, he's not.'

'How about just now?' Sally asked.

'He wasn't sneaking up on us . . .'

'I say he was.'

'Home free . . .' they heard Douglas call.

'Doesn't he remind you of somebody?' Sally whispered to Andrea.

'Who?'

'Mr Zavodsky.'

'Not especially.'

'Picture him with a small black moustache and slick dark hair . . .'

'Oh yeah . . .' Andrea said, 'I guess he does look a little like my grandfather . . . come on . . . let's run in . . .'

Dear Mr Zavodsky,
I know you are in disguise. You have shaved off
your moustache and let your hair grow in grey but
I am not so easy to fool. I happen to be one of the
best detectives around and I am working on your
case. So watch it!

They were at the beach on the Saturday before
Thanksgiving. Mom had been dieting and with her
hair in an upsweep and dressed in her new bathing
suit she looked taller and slimmer than before. Her
skin was very white so she always sat under an
umbrella or in the shade of a palm tree. She never
went near the water because when she'd been a little
girl her father had thrown her into the ocean in
Atlantic City, saying that was the best way to learn
to swim. She'd been so scared she'd nearly drowned
and never tried again.

Sally couldn't imagine a father throwing his child
into the water. Certainly her father would never do
such a thing. And if Ma Fanny had been along that
day, long ago, in Atlantic City, she never would have
allowed Grandfather to throw Mom in. Sally was sure
of that. Sally hardly remembered her grandfather. He
had died when she was just three years old, the year
before Uncle Eddie and two years before Uncle Abe.
Her other grandmother had died when Sally was
eight, the same year as Aunt Ruth, Daddy's older
sister, which was six months before Aunt Lena,
Daddy's younger sister.

Ma Fanny liked the beach. She had just one

bathing suit and Sally admired it. It had purple flowers all over and a skirt bottom. Sally found it much more interesting than Mom's new suit which was plain black. Ma Fanny didn't swim but she did get wet. She'd stand at the ocean's edge and splash herself and when she did the loose flesh of her arms wiggled.

On this day Sally and Andrea had finally convinced their mothers to let them go to the public bathhouse to change before lunch. But they'd had to promise not to use the toilets there.

'Douglas looked down my bathing suit this morning,' Andrea told Sally, as she stepped out of her wet suit.

'What for?' Sally asked.

'To see my tits . . . what do you think?'

'So how come you let him?' Sally dried carefully between her toes.

'I didn't let him . . . he just did it.'

'I don't believe you,' Sally said.

'I don't *care* what you believe. It's true! You're just jealous because you don't have tits yet.'

'I have them,' Sally said.

'You have buttons, that's all . . . you're still a child.'

'If I'm such a child how come you play potsy with me every day after school?'

'That's different,' Andrea said. 'You're the best potsy player in our house.'

Sally smiled. At least Andrea admitted *that*. She *was* the potsy champion of 1330 Pennsylvania Avenue and she intended to keep it that way.

108

'I've already kissed two boys,' Andrea said on their way back from the bathhouse. 'Did you know that?'

'Real kisses . . .' Sally asked, 'like in the movies?'

'One was and the other wasn't,' Andrea said.

'Tell me about the one that was . . .'

'Well . . . he was this friend of my cousin Gary's from Long Island . . . he's in eighth grade now but this was over the summer . . . he thought I was thirteen . . . at least . . .'

'What'd it feel like?' Sally asked.

'Oh, you know . . . nothing much . . . he put his face real close to mine and then I closed my eyes . . .'

'Was he *that* ugly?'

'No! You're supposed to close your eyes . . . you never watch . . . that's bad manners . . .'

'Oh.'

'And then he put his lips on mine and we kissed.'

'Did you like it?' Sally kicked at the sand. If you did it just right you could make it squeak.

'I told you . . . it was all right . . . I didn't especially like *him* though . . . Latin lovers are the best . . .'

'How can you tell if a lover is Latin?' Sally asked.

'Oh, he'll have dark, flashing eyes and he'll talk with an accent.'

'You talk with an accent,' Sally said.

'I do not!'

'You do too! You say *mothah* and *fathah* instead of *mother* and *father*.'

'That's not an accent!' Andrea said, annoyed. 'Everyone from New York talks that way. You sound just as strange to me, if you want to know the truth. Besides, I thought you loved the movies . . . I thought Esther Williams was your favourite movie star . . .'

'She is,' Sally said, 'but what's that got to do with it?'

'Because you should know about Latin lovers . . . her boyfriends are all Latin.'

'The ones who stand around and sing?' Sally asked, surprised.

'Yes . . . and the ones who kiss her . . . like Fernando Lamas . . .'

'He's Latin?'

'Of course . . . you should pay closer attention to details,' Andrea said.

'From now on I will.' Sally thought about Peter Hornstein. He had dark eyes. She wasn't sure if they were flashing though. She'd have to pay closer attention to details, as Andrea said. Maybe Peter Hornstein would grow up to be a Latin lover. And he liked her. Barbara said so. Wouldn't Andrea be surprised to hear that Sally had her own Latin lover!

During supper that night, Sally said, 'Mom . . . where's Latin?'

'Latin what?' Mom asked.

'You know . . . Latin . . .'

'There's no such place as Latin,' Mom said.

'Then where do Latin lovers come from?'

'Who's been filling your head with Latin lovers?' Mom asking, laughing.

110

'Nobody special . . . me and Andrea were just talking.'

'She means Latin America, I guess,' Mom said.

'Where's that?'

'South . . .'

'Like here . . . like Miami Beach, you mean?' Sally asked.

'No,' Mom said, 'south of the border . . . more like Cuba or Mexico or South America.'

'Oh.' Sally picked up her lamb chop bone. She liked to suck on it after the meat was gone.

'Latin lovers . . .' Douglas mumbled, chuckling.

Sally didn't answer him out loud but to herself she said, you're just jealous because you'll never be one, so ha ha on you, Douglas.

Mom was singing in the shower. Sally hadn't seen or heard her so happy in a long time, not since before Douglas had his accident. Tonight Mom was going to Miami, to the airport, to meet Daddy's plane. It was due in very late.

Ma Fanny was in the tiny kitchen, baking.

'Ummm . . . smells good,' Sally said.

'I don't trust this oven,' Ma Fanny said. 'I hope it doesn't ruin my pie or God forbid, my turkey.'

'Oh, Ma Fanny . . . you're such a good cook . . . you couldn't ruin anything if you tried.'

'Maybe yes, maybe no,' Ma Fanny said.

'I'll knock on wood for you,' Sally suggested, 'just to make sure everything comes out delicious.'

111

'You knock on wood *after* it comes out delicious . . . not before,' Ma Fanny said.

Sally thumped the wooden table anyway.

When she and Douglas were in bed and all the lights were out, Sally said, 'I wish Daddy's plane landed earlier so they wouldn't have to stay overnight in that hotel near the airport.'

'That's not why they're staying in a hotel,' Douglas said.

'It's not?'

'No.'

'Then, why?' Sally asked.

'So they can be alone.'

'But why would they want to be alone?'

'You know . . .'

'No, I don't.'

'So they can do it,' Douglas said.

'Do what?'

'You're so dumb sometimes . . .' Douglas sounded disgusted. 'Don't you know anything?'

'How can I know anything if nobody ever tells me!'

'Oh . . . go to sleep.'

Sally thought about Fernando Lamas kissing Esther Williams, then about her father kissing her mother the same way. Not that she'd ever seen them do that. But it was possible, she supposed. Could that be it then? They wanted to be alone so they could kiss

for a long time? Maybe. But that seemed so silly . . .
couldn't they kiss just as well right here . . . in the
Murphy bed?

Chapter 12

'Doey-bird!' Sally cried, jumping into her father's arms. 'I'm so glad you're here.' She kissed him on both sides of his face.

'My little gal,' Daddy said. 'How I've missed my little gal . . .' He hugged her hard and returned her kisses.

'Hi, Dad,' Douglas said.

Her father put Sally down, then hugged Douglas. 'How are you, son?'

'Pretty good. I invented a coconut retriever . . . you want to see it?'

'Sure . . . just as soon as I get settled.' He rumpled Douglas's hair. 'Growing taller and taller . . .'

'Yeah . . . my pants are getting too short again.'

'Arnold!' Ma Fanny called, rushing out of the kitchen, wiping her hands on her apron.

'Ma Fanny!' Daddy said, holding her at arm's length for a minute. 'Just look at that tan! You look about twenty-five.' He pulled her to him.

'Always with the compliments,' Ma Fanny said, laughing.

'For you . . . why not?' Daddy said.

On the radio, comedians like Bob Hope and Jack Benny were always telling mother-in-law jokes but Sally knew that her father and Ma Fanny really liked each other. They're much more alike than Ma Fanny and Mom, Sally thought. How strange, since they aren't even blood relatives.

Mom stood in the doorway, watching and smiling. She has such a pretty smile, Sally thought. If only she'd show it more often.

Daddy had presents for all of them – a handbag for Ma Fanny, a gold necklace for Mom, a special tool kit for Douglas and for Sally, the Jolly Roger game. She wasn't as surprised as she pretended to be. There were so many things to tell her father, so many things to show him. She'd never catch up in a week and then he'd be gone again.

They sat down to Thanksgiving dinner at four o'clock. After she'd tasted the turkey, Ma Fanny said, 'It's too dry.'

'No, it's fine,' Mom told her and Daddy added, 'It's delicious!'

'I overcooked it . . . half an hour earlier it would have been perfect.' Tears came to her eyes.

'It's good this way,' Mom said, but Ma Fanny had already pushed back her chair and was heading for the kitchen.

Daddy and Mom exchanged looks, then he got up and went after Ma Fanny.

'Just keep eating,' Mom told Sally and Douglas, but Sally didn't feel hungry anymore. She could hear her father talking softly and Ma Fanny blowing her nose.

In a little while Daddy and Ma Fanny came back to the table. He had his arm around her. 'I'm sorry,'

Ma Fanny said, taking her seat. 'I was being silly . . . who cares about the turkey as long as we're all well . . .' She sniffled. 'I just wish Bette and Jack could be with us.'

'Next year,' Mom said, patting Ma Fanny's hand. 'Next year we'll all be together.'

'Knock wood,' Ma Fanny said.

'Anyway,' Sally said, ' . . . who likes juicy turkey?'

They all laughed but this time Sally was hoping they would. Suddenly she felt hungry again.

The next night her parents were going to a night-club with somebody named Wiskoff that Daddy had met on the plane. Mom wore a dark blue dress that rustled as she walked and high-heeled shoes. New rhinestone combs held her upsweep hairdo in place. Sally sat on the Murphy bed and watched as Mom put some more rouge on her cheeks, went over her lips a second time and dabbed a drop of perfume behind each ear. 'You smell good,' Sally said. 'Like lilies of the valley.'

'It's called *White Shoulders*,' Mom said. 'It's my favourite . . . here, I'll put some behind your ears too.'

'Ummm . . . I like that,' Sally said, wondering if Latin lovers would be attracted to it. Maybe she'd try it out on Peter Hornstein.

Sally went into the living-room. 'Smell me,' she said to Douglas, putting her face close to his nose.

'Uck! Get out of here . . . you stink!'

'I do not.'

'That is a matter of opinion!' Douglas said.

'Do I get my treatment now?' Daddy asked, putting down the *Miami Herald*, 'or should I wait until I get home?'

'I'll probably be asleep by then,' Sally told him, arranging herself on his lap. 'I better give it to you now.' She put her face next to his. 'Do you like the way I smell?'

'Like *White Shoulders*,' Daddy said.

'How'd you know?'

'I've been enjoying it for a long time.'

'Oh . . .' Sally gave him a sliding kiss, up one cheek, across his forehead, down the other cheek, three quick hugs, and a butterfly on the nose.

'That was very nice,' Daddy said. 'I've really missed my treatments.'

'Me too,' Sally said. 'Doey-bird . . .'

'Yes . . .'

'How are you feeling?'

'Very, very nice.' He closed his eyes for a minute.

Sally traced his eyelids with her fingertip. 'I mean, how are you feeling, in general?'

'In general, I'm feeling just fine.' He opened his eyes and looked concerned. 'Why do you ask?'

'I was just wondering . . .'

'How about you?' Daddy said. 'Are you feeling all right?'

'Me?' Sally said. 'I'm fine. You know that. Douglas is the one you should be asking.'

'I thought maybe you were trying to tell me something.'

'No . . . nothing like that.' But inside Sally was

saying, I am trying to tell you something, Doey . . . please make it through your bad year . . . please don't die!'

'Have a wonderful time,' Ma Fanny said, when Mom and Daddy were ready to leave. 'And don't worry about a thing. Sally's going to teach me and Dougie to play Jolly Roger. Who knows . . . maybe I'll like it better than rummy.'

At ten, Sally, Douglas and Ma Fanny got ready for bed.

Sally fell asleep quickly and had a strange dream.

She is sitting in a movie theatre on Lincoln Road. The lights dim, the curtain rises, the music begins and the title of the motion picture everyone has been waiting for flashes onto the silver screen in glorious techicolour. *The White Shoulders*, starring Sally Jane Freedman as Lila and Mr Zavodsky as Adolf Hitler. You know right away it's going to be a war story because of the soldiers on the street. Lila is one of them. She is petting a turkey. All the soldiers are talking and laughing because it is rest hour. But then the whistle blows and it is time to get back to the battle.

Good luck, they say to Lila. *Remember, you're the only one who can do it . . . we're counting on you.*

One soldier lingers after the others are gone. *Oh, Peter . . . Peter . . .* Lila sighs. *I'm frightened . . . not for myself, but for you. If I fail . . . if I . . .*

No ifs or buts, my darling, Peter whispers, holding

Lila close. *Soon it will be all over . . . soon we will be together again.*

And will there be a parade? Lila asks.

Yes, my darling . . . a parade for you.

I'll try my best, Peter . . . I only hope that's enough.

It's all anyone can ask, Peter says, with tears in his eyes. *Goodbye, Lila . . . for just a little while.*

Goodbye, Peter . . . we'll meet again in Latin. They kiss.

The turkey flies away.

And now Lila is alone on the street. She waits, her hand in her pocket, ready for action. At last he approaches. Adolf Hitler, monster of monsters.

What is that delicious smell? he asks, his nostrils twitching like a rabbit's.

It is me, Lila says in a husky voice.

He runs toward her. *Such a smell . . . I can't stand it . . . it is too good.*

It is called White Shoulders, Lila says, *an old family perfume, handed down from my mother and before her, my grandmother . . .*

Hitler's face is almost touching Lila's. She feels sick to her stomach but she has a job to do. She whips her pistol out of her pocket, points it at Hitler's gut and says, *From all of us on the other side . . .* and she pulls the trigger . . .

Sally awakened hours later to voices in the hall. It was Mom and Daddy. Mom was laughing and saying something silly. Something that sounded like *willya . . . willya . . . willya.* Daddy was laughing too, but more quietly. She heard the key in the door and then they were inside the apartment. Daddy said, 'Shush, Louise . . . you'll wake the kids . . .'

'Willya . . . willya . . . willya . . .'

Ma Fanny snored and Douglas rolled over in bed and hit the wall.

Sally lay very still but she opened her eyes. Daddy was holding Mom up, with his arm around her waist. Mom was carrying one of her shoes and wearing the other. 'Willya . . . willya . . . willya . . .' she said, laughing harder.

'Shush . . . come on, Lou . . .'

'What's wrong with Mom?' Sally whispered to her father.

'Too much champagne . . . go back to sleep now.'

'Willya . . . willya . . . willya . . .'

Sally pulled the bedsheet up around her ears and closed her eyes.

In the morning Mom couldn't get out of bed. Daddy made an icepack for her head and brought her a glass of tomato juice. She wasn't laughing any more.

Daddy took Sally and Douglas to the beach. He helped Sally collect shells, built a beautiful sand castle, then fooled around with them in the ocean. Later, he sat on their blanket and played gin rummy with Andrea's father, while Sally and Andrea ran off to practise cartwheels.

Sally was soaking in the tub. Her shoulders were sunburned again and Ma Fanny had put some vinegar in her bath water, to take the sting away. Her parents were in the sleeping alcove, arguing, because Mr Wiskoff had invited them all out to dinner and Mom didn't want to go.

Sally could hear everything. That was the good thing about this apartment. At home, in New Jersey, her parents could talk privately and Sally couldn't make out a word. She had to imagine it all.

'Seven hours on a plane and they're your best friends?'

'I didn't say best friends . . . I said *friends* . . . why can't you get that straight? The other night . . .'

'The other night I got drunk,' Mom said. 'For the first time in my life . . . I still don't see how you could have let me . . .'

'Oh, come on, Lou . . . you enjoyed it . . . and they enjoyed you . . . you should try letting go more often . . .'

'I'm telling you . . . I just can't face them tonight.'

'Because you're embarrassed?'

'Partly . . . and I certainly don't think it's wise to expose the children to them.'

'Nobody has to know they're not married,' Daddy said.

'It's not just that . . . they aren't our kind of people, Arnold.'

'Do we always have to associate with the same kinds of people?'

'I'd rather go out with the Rubins . . . they asked us to join them.'

'We've already accepted Ted's invitation.'

'You could call and say I'm sick.'

'You're being unreasonable, Louise.'

'I have a feeling about him . . .'

'Look . . . he gambles a little and he plays the market in a big way . . . but so what?'

'I don't know,' Mom said. 'I'm just not comfortable with them.'

'You could try . . . for me . . .'

'All right . . . I'll try . . . it's just that we have so little time together . . . I hate sharing you with them.'

'Lou . . . Lou . . .'

Sally listened hard but she couldn't hear anything after that.

Daddy wanted Ma Fanny to join them too, but she said she had her card game and he should please understand that she couldn't disappoint her friends. So Sally and Douglas and Mom and Daddy took a taxi to The Park Avenue Restaurant near Lincoln Road.

The Wiskoffs were waiting at the table. Daddy introduced them, saying, 'Ted . . . Vicki . . . these are my children, Douglas and Sally.'

Mr Wiskoff stood up and shook hands with Douglas. He was tall, with slick black hair, turning grey around the ears. He wore a dark, striped suit and in the middle of his tie was a diamond stick pin. A red silk handkerchief showed out of the top of his jacket pocket and Sally wondered if he actually used it to blow his nose. 'Hooloo, sweetheart,' he said to Sally. 'You're as adorable as your Daddy promised.'

He leaned across Sally then, and kissed Mom's cheek. 'How're you doing, doll?' he asked her.

All this time Douglas was staring at Vicki. Sally didn't blame him. Because Vicki looked just like Rita Hayworth, the movie star, with long red hair and a wide, beautiful smile. She was wearing a green silk dress, the same colour as her eyes, and more jewellery than Sally had ever seen, all of it sparkling.

Sally got to sit next to her and could see that Douglas would have given anything to trade places, including his orange marble, because Sally could look right down the front of Vicki's dress and Vicki wasn't wearing anything under it!

When the waiter took their order, Mr Wiskoff said, 'And a bottle of your best champagne for the doll over there.' He nodded in Mom's direction. 'She really enjoys her bubbly.'

Mom held up her hand. 'Not tonight, Ted . . . really.'

Mr Wiskoff winked at the waiter. 'Bring it anyway . . .'

'Yes, sir.'

Sally ordered fruit cup supreme, roast beef, mashed potatoes, carrots, and chocolate ice cream. When he served dessert, the waiter brought a big silver bowl of whipped cream to their table and they each got to spoon as much as they wanted on to their plates. Sally loved whipped cream, especially over chocolate ice cream, but she wouldn't have minded it plain either. Just a plate of whipped cream would do any day. Nothing tasted as good. This was definitely her favourite restaurant. In the whole world there couldn't be another restaurant this good. She felt just a little bit guilty, thinking of all the starving children in Europe.

After the coffee had been served Vicki said, 'I've got to go to the little girls' room . . . anyone need to join me?'

'No, thanks,' Mom said, but Sally quickly answered, 'I will . . . I mean, I do,' and she stood up and followed Vicki.

A lot of people turned to look at them as they crossed the dining-room and Sally knew it was because of Vicki, not her. As Vicki walked, her backside wiggled from side to side and her breasts bounced up and down. It was exciting just to be near her.

In the Ladies' Room, Vicki sat down at a small dressing table and pulled a make-up kit out of her purse. Sally stood next to her, watching. Vicki put green eye shadow on her lids. 'You want to try some, honey?' she asked.

'Okay,' Sally said.

'Very nice,' Vicki told her as she rubbed it on to Sally's lids. 'It brings out the colour of your eyes.'

'But my eyes are brown, not green.'

'Brown and green are a good combination.' Vicki zipped up her make-up bag and shook out her hair.

Sally shook hers, too.

'Do you like my ring?' Vicki asked. She held it to her mouth and breathed hard on it. 'It's twelve carats . . .'

'I like carrots,' Sally said.

'Me too.' Vicki laughed. 'My necklace is emerald and diamond. Isn't it pretty?'

'Yes, very . . .'

'Would you undo the clasp for me, honey . . . I need to wash it.'

Sally stood behind Vicki and undid the clasp of her necklace. Vicki caught it as it dropped, and spread it out on the dressing table. Then she took another bag out of her purse and unzipped it. She pulled out a small bottle and a soft, white cloth.

'My mother has combs for her hair that sparkle like that,' Sally said, admiring Vicki's necklace.

'That's nice, honey . . . but these are the *real* things . . . now, I'm going to show you how to wash diamonds . . . every girl should know how to do it the right way . . . watch carefully . . .' Vicki poured some liquid on to the white cloth. 'You see how nice they look now? You see how they sparkle?'

'Yes. Did Mr Wiskoff give them to you?'

'Of course! Teddy and I have been together almost six years.' Sally noticed that she didn't say *married*.

'I do for him and he does for me,' Vicki said. 'That's the way it should be . . . don't you think?'

'Oh, yes!' Sally said. 'That's the way it is with my parents too.'

'Really?' Vicki sounded surprised.

'Yes . . . like tonight, my mother didn't want to come but my father . . .' Sally put her hand to her mouth and blushed. 'I mean . . .'

'I know just what you mean,' Vicki said.

'But, I . . .'

'It's all right. I'll pretend I never heard a word. You know something, Sally?'

'No . . . what?'

'I like you!'

'I like you too.'

'How would you like to wear one of my bracelets for a little while?'

'Well, I don't know . . . I have my own . . . you see . . .' She held out her wrist so Vicki could see her shell bracelet. 'I bought it in Woolworth's . . . they're real shells too . . . from the beach.'

'Very pretty,' Vicki said. 'I guess you don't need mine after all, then.'

'I guess not,' Sally said. 'But thank you anyway.'

Vicki was going through her make-up bag again, deciding which lipstick to use. She chose a bright pink one, applied it, then blotted her lips with a tissue.

'Is Mr Wiskoff, by any chance, Latin?' Sally asked.

'Latin?' Vicki said.

'Yes . . . from Cuba or Mexico or someplace south of the border?'

Vicki laughed. 'Teddy is New York all the way, honey. He's a very important man back east . . . and don't you forget it . . . you've had dinner with Big Ted Wiskoff and that means a lot!'

'Wash that goo off your eyes before you go to sleep,' Mom said, in the taxi, on the way back to their apartment.

'Do I have to?' Sally asked.

'Yes!'

'But it looks so pretty.'

'Pretty awful!' Douglas said.

Sally gave him an elbow in the ribs. 'Do you know they call Mr Wiskoff, *Big Ted?*' Sally asked her father.

Mom answered, 'And not because he's tall, I'll bet.'

'I really liked him,' Douglas said. 'And that Mrs Wiskoff . . . what a dish!'

'She showed me how to wash diamonds,' Sally told them.

'That's wonderful!' Mom said. 'Every girl should know how to wash diamonds.'

'That's exactly what Vicki said!'

Mom snorted and looked out of the window.

Daddy laughed. 'Did you enjoy dinner, kids?'

'Oh, yeah . . . it was great,' Douglas answered.

'And all that whipped cream,' Sally said. 'Yum!'

When they got out of the taxi they saw the Goodyear Blimp in the sky. It was all lit up. Douglas said, 'Oh, boy . . . would I like to fly around in that!'

Mom said, 'Some people don't have enough trouble . . . they have to go looking for it.'

'Was tonight an adventure, Doey?' Sally asked. She was already tucked into bed and Daddy sat on the edge, waiting for his treatment.

'I'll say . . .'

'I thought so.'

'I'm glad you had a good time, Sal . . .'

'Mmm . . . I really did.'

When her mother came over to kiss her goodnight Sally reached up and put her arms around Mom's neck. 'You know something . . . I wouldn't want a mother who looks like Vicki . . . she's nice and all that but I don't think she'd know how to love a kid the way she loves her diamonds . . .' She kissed Mom's cheek.

Mom hugged her back. 'Thank you, Sally . . . I really needed to hear that tonight.'

Chapter 13

Dear Doey,

I miss you already! I hope you had a good trip home. Next time I think you should fly National Airlines because Barbara's mother works for them. You remember who Barbara is, don't you?

I forgot to tell you something very important when you were here. My teacher, Miss Swetnick, goes out with Peter Hornstein's brother. Peter Hornstein sits behind me in class. I also forgot to ask if you could fix my front tooth like my teacher's. It looks very pretty when she smiles.

I am still trying to get my first E for excellent in penmanship. Doesn't my writing look better? I don't make my o's like a's any more.

Well, that's it for now. Send my love to Aunt Bette, Uncle Jack and Miss Kay.
Your loving and only daughter,
S.J.F.

She folded the letter and placed it in an envelope. Then she took out another piece of paper. As long as she was writing letters she might as well write one to *him* too.

Dear Mr Zavodsky,
I had a dream about you. I am almost sure I know who you really are. Give yourself up before I report

you to the police. I will be watching and waiting.
Don't think you can get away with this disguise of
yours. Nobody feels sorry for you just because you
lost.

Sally and Andrea were sitting at the edge of the goldfish pool in the courtyard, playing the initial game. Omar had his front paws on the edge of the pool and was peering over the side.

'You can look but don't touch,' Andrea warned Omar. 'No goldfish for you!'

Omar purred and stuck his tail straight up in the air.

'Look at that,' Sally said. 'I never saw him do that before.'

'Oh, sure . . . it means he wants affection.'

'How do you know?'

'I read it in this book called *Getting To Know Your Cat*,' Andrea said. 'When they stick their tails up like that you should pet them.' She reached out and stroked Omar's back. 'It's your turn . . .'

Sally petted Omar too.

'Not for that!' Andrea said, annoyed. 'For the initial game.'

'Oh,' Sally said, ' . . . okay, I'm thinking of a famous person and his initials are A.H.'

'A.H.,' Andrea repeated, 'let's see . . . is he a movie star?'

'Nope.'

'A radio personality?'

'Nope.'

'Uh . . . a political figure?'

'I guess you could say that . . .'

'Let's see . . .' Andrea put her finger to her lip and looked up at the sky. 'I've got it . . . Admiral Halsey!'

'Nope,' Sally said. 'But did I ever tell you that I saw Admiral Halsey's parade when he came home from the war?'

'You did?'

'Yes . . . I threw confetti and everything . . . but that's not who I'm thinking of . . .'

'Well,' Andrea said, 'then I give up . . . I can't think of anybody else with those initials . . .'

'How about Adolf Hitler?' Sally was pleased that she'd stumped Andrea.

'Adolf Hitler!' Andrea said, and she leaned over the side of the goldfish pool and spat into it. 'How can you even say that name without spitting?'

'I never spit,' Sally said.

'Well, you should . . . every time you say that name . . . every time you even hear it you should spit . . . he made lampshades out of Jewish people's skin!'

'He did?' Sally leaned over and spat into the pool too. 'There,' she said, wiping her mouth with the back of her hand.

'And don't you ever use that filthy name on me again,' Andrea said, 'or I'll never play the initial game with you!'

'All right,' Sally said. 'I'm thinking of a . . .' She was interrupted by a high, shrill scream, coming from the side yard. Both girls jumped up and ran to see what was happening. It was Mrs Richter, a small, thin woman with white hair. Other people rushed outside to see what the commotion was about. Through it all Mrs Richter kept screaming, with one hand clutching her chest and the other pointing to the bushes.

Mr Koner, the landlord, who also lived in their building, said, 'Tell us what's wrong . . .'

Mrs Richter just shook her head, took a breath and let out another scream.

'Try to tell us what it is . . .' Mr Koner said. 'How can we help you if you won't tell us . . .'

Mrs Richter began to cry and talk at the same time. 'It's the second one this week . . . and two last week . . . that makes four . . . and the week before another one . . . that makes five . . . my heart isn't what it used to be . . . I can't take much more of it . . . it's that cat's fault . . .'

'What cat?' Mr Koner asked.

'That cat!' Mrs Richter said. 'That white cat . . .' She pointed to Omar. 'I've seen him running through these bushes. I've seen him chasing birds.'

Everyone looked towards the bushes and there, on the ground, lay a bird's head. The crowd that had gathered began to chatter.

Andrea grew pale and scooped Omar into her arms. 'It's *not* Omar,' she told everyone. 'He gets enough to eat at home . . . he doesn't need any old birds!'

'You keep him locked up . . . you hear?' Mrs Richter shouted. 'Because if I see him again . . .'

Andrea turned and ran back to the courtyard. Sally followed. Andrea held Omar to her. 'It wasn't you . . . I know it wasn't you . . .' she told him, kissing his face. 'I love you, Omar . . . don't you listen to that old witch . . .'

'Everybody knows she's crazy,' Sally said. 'Just ask my grandmother . . . she'll tell you . . . just because she's from Boston she thinks she's so great . . . she won't even play rummy with the rest of the ladies . . .'

'I hate her!' Andrea said.

Sally was thoughtful for a minute. 'You could get Omar a collar with bells . . . then he'd scare the birds away and Mrs Richter wouldn't be able to blame him anymore.'

Andrea looked at Sally. 'That's a very good idea . . . sometimes you really surprise me . . . for a fifth-grader you're pretty smart.'

Sally smiled.

They took Omar upstairs, then walked to the Five and Dime, where they chose a blue collar with three tiny bells.

'Don't you think this collar will go nicely with his eyes?' Andrea asked.

'Yes . . . he'll look really pretty in it.'

'Let's hurry home and try it on him,' Andrea said.

'Okay . . . I just want to stop at the fountain for a drink of water . . . I'm so thirsty . . .'

'Yeah . . . me too . . . it's really hot today,' Andrea said. 'We could stop at the corner and get a glass of orange juice instead.'

'The orange juice at the corner has too many pieces on it.'

'It's not pieces . . . it's pulp,' Andrea said. 'I love my juice pulpy.'

'Not me . . . pulp gags me.'

'You have to open your throat wide.'

'I can't.'

'You could ask the man to strain it for you,' Andrea suggested.

'I did once . . . I was with my mother and the man behind the counter said he wouldn't do it because all the vitamins are in the pulp and why should my mother pay for a fresh orange juice with no vitamins . . . so if you don't mind I'll just get a drink of water . . .'

'I don't mind.'

They walked to the drinking fountain at the back of the store and Sally stood on tiptoe. Andrea held the button down for her. As Sally was drinking a woman came up from behind and yanked her away.

'Hey . . .' Andrea said.

'What's the matter with you girls?' the woman asked. 'Can't you read?' She pointed to a sign above the fountain: *Coloured*. 'Your fountain is over there.' She spun Sally around by the shoulders. 'You see . . . it says *White* . . . what would your mothers say if they knew what you'd been doing? God only knows what you might pick up drinking from this fountain . . . you better thank your lucky stars I came along when I did. Now here,' she said, reaching into her purse for a Kleenex. She handed it to Sally. 'You wipe your mouth off real good and from now on be more careful . . .'

Sally was shaking. When the woman was gone she turned to Andrea. 'Did you know they had two fountains?'

'No,' Andrea said. 'I never even thought about it.'

'Me neither . . . but I know Negro people have to sit in the back of the bus here.'

'Everybody with dark skin has to . . .' Andrea said. 'That's why my mother always makes me sit up front.'

'Do you think that's fair?'

'I don't know, but my mother says you have to follow the rules.'

'So does mine.'

They began to walk home slowly.

'We had a Negro lady who came in to clean three times a week in New Jersey,' Sally said, 'and here we have one every Friday . . . she's half Seminole Indian . . . my mother told me. She has dark skin but she eats off our dishes and drinks from our glasses and all that . . .'

'It's not the same thing,' Andrea said.

'I don't see the difference . . . she's very nice . . . and she's got the prettiest name . . . Precious Redwine . . . isn't that a beautiful name?'

'Yes, but I wouldn't want it,' Andrea said. 'Nobody in Brooklyn has a name like that.'

'Nobody in New Jersey has either.'

Dear Doey-bird,

Right now Douglas is listening to the radio. Jack Armstrong, All American Boy *is on. I haven't been following Jack Armstrong lately so I don't know what's happening. Did I tell you that I'm not as scared of* The Shadow *as I used to be? I still don't like it when he laughs and says* The Shadow knows . . . *but I don't have to stuff my ears with cotton the way I do when Douglas listens to* Inner Sanctum.

This afternoon me and Andrea went to the Five and Dime and I took a drink from the wrong water fountain. They have two of them here. One is marked White *and the other is marked* Coloured. *What would happen if a person with dark skin, like a Negro or a Seminole Indian, took a drink from our fountain? Do they really have different germs? Since you went to Dental College I'm sure you know these things . . .*

Dear Sally,

In your last letter you raised some questions that are very hard to answer. I have always believed that people have more similarities than differences, regardless of the colour of their skin. While the south continues to practise outright segregation, the north is not much better. We just don't admit we do it. For instance, how many Negro children were in your school in New Jersey? . . .

Dear Doey-bird,
One. He was in sixth grade. And you forgot to tell
me if people with dark skin have different germs
in their mouths. And can they give trench mouth to
white people? I have decided that if I ever have a
daughter I will name her Precious. Don't you think
that's a beautiful name? I wish it could be my
name even though Precious Redwine sounds a lot
better than Precious Freedman . . .

Dear Sally,
Trench mouth has nothing to do with the colour of
your skin. Anyone can get it. As for germs in
people's mouths, we are all the same . . .

Dear Doey-bird,
Then why does the Five and Dime have two
fountains and why do they drink only from theirs
and we drink only from ours? And you didn't tell
me what you think about my favourite name . . .

Dear Sally,
Your questions are very hard to answer. At the
moment it is simply the way things are. I doubt
that they will remain that way forever, but for now,
you have to abide by the rules. I'm glad that you're
questioning those rules though. Yes, I think Precious
is a lovely name and that is exactly what you are,
even though we call you Sally . . .

Chapter 14

Sally, Shelby and Andrea were walking home from school. Sally was careful not to step on any cracks in the sidewalk. Shelby went out of her way to step on *every* one. When they reached the corner Shelby said, 'Bye . . . see you tomorrow . . . I've got to go to the dentist this afternoon.' She went up the walk to her house.

As soon as she was gone, Andrea said, 'Can you keep a secret, Sally?'

'Yes.'

'You're sure?'

'Of course!' Sally said.

Andrea stood still and faced Sally. 'Okay . . . I've decided to tell you and *only* you because you came up with the idea for Omar's collar . . . but if anybody ever finds out . . .'

'I can keep a secret!' Sally insisted.

'Okay.' Andrea took a big breath. 'I'm in love.'

'You are?'

Andrea started walking again. 'Yes . . . hopelessly.'

'Is that good or bad?' Sally had to hurry to keep up with her, skipping over every line in the pavement.

'It all depends,' Andrea said.

'On what?'

Andrea shrugged, as if she wasn't sure herself.

'Who is he?' Sally asked.

'He's called Georgia Blue Eyes . . . he's new . . . he's in Mrs Wingate's portable.'

'Oh . . . that's right next to Shelby's . . . maybe she knows him . . .'

'This is a secret, remember?'

'Don't worry . . . I won't give you away,' Sally said. 'What's his real name?'

'I don't know . . . but he's from Georgia and he has the most beautiful blue eyes you ever saw.'

'Nicer than Omar's?'

'Omar is a cat.' Andrea said this as if Sally didn't already know.

'I thought you liked Latin lovers best . . . with dark and flashing eyes.'

'I do sometimes,' Andrea said quietly, and then she became annoyed. 'Will you stop jumping like that . . . you look like a kangaroo.'

'I don't want to step on any cracks.'

'Don't tell me you believe that garbage about your mother's back . . . that's the silliest superstition.'

'I don't believe it.'

'Then stop jumping!'

'I like to jump.'

'Sometimes you act younger than a fifth grader . . . you know that . . . and I *was* going to ask you to come to the park with me this afternoon . . . but now I'm not so sure . . .'

'And sometimes I act older . . . you said so yourself.' Sally waited for Andrea to agree with her. When she didn't, Sally asked, 'So what's at the park today?'

'Georgia Blue Eyes . . . I heard he's playing ball there this afternoon.'

'Oh,' Sally said and she stopped jumping.

'Can I go to the park with Andrea?' Sally asked her mother. 'Please . . . I'll be very careful.'

'Walking or on bicycles?' Mom asked.

'Bicycles . . . but I'll watch out for cars . . . I promise . . . please . . .'

'All right,' Mom said. 'But be back by five . . . that means you have to leave the park no later than quarter to . . .'

'Okay . . .'

She and Andrea rode their bicycles to Flamingo Park. When they got to a field where a bunch of boys were playing ball Andrea's face flushed and she said, 'There he is!'

'Which one?' Sally asked.

'On first base . . . isn't he the most beautiful boy you've ever seen?'

'I don't know.'

'How can you not know? Look at that hair . . . oh, I'd love to run my fingers through it.'

'He might have nits.'

'Are you crazy?' Andrea asked.

'Some people do, you know.'

'Not *nice* people.'

'Even them . . .' Sally said.

'Never! Nits are what dirty disgusting people get from not shampooing and Georgia Blue Eyes isn't dirty *or* disgusting!'

140

'Maybe . . .' Sally paused for a minute, not
to go deeper into that subject. 'So, you want to
around or just sit here and watch?' she asked Andrea.

'Hmm . . . I guess we should ride around for a
while. We can circle the field . . . that way he might
notice me.'

They rode around three times but if Georgia Blue
Eyes noticed Andrea he kept it to himself. Then
Andrea decided they should ride around the rest of
the park and come back to the field later, when
Georgia Blue Eyes wasn't quite so busy.

They rode past the tennis courts, past the food
stand and through the wooded area. Mr Zavodsky
was there, sitting on a bench, reading *The Forward*.
Andrea called, 'Yoo hoo . . . Mr Zavodsky . . .' and
when he looked up she waved.

Sally caught Andrea's arm and held it down. 'Cut
that out!' Andrea said, shaking Sally off. 'Got any
candy today?' Andrea called to Mr Zavodsky.

'For you . . . always . . .' He beckoned to her.

'Don't go,' Sally said, under her breath.

'Why not?' Andrea asked.

'I don't trust him.'

'Why?'

'He offers us candy and we're . . . practically
strangers . . .'

'We are not . . . he knows us.'

'He doesn't know *me* at all!'

'Oh, Sally . . . quit being such a jerk!' Andrea got
off her bicycle, kicked down the stand and ran across
the grass.

141

You monster! Sally thought. *Reading* The Forward, *a Yiddish newspaper . . . pretending to be Jewish . . . and after you've made lampshades out of Jews' skin! I hate you . . . I hate you . . . you think you're so smart, coming to Miami Beach to retire, like everybody else . . . I'll bet you think this is a great hiding place . . . well, you're wrong . . .*

Andrea came back with a handful of rock candy. 'Want some?' she asked Sally.

'No!' Sally said and rode off.

Andrea caught up with her. 'What's wrong with you this time?'

Sally didn't answer. She just kept pedalling.

'Are you sick or something . . . you look funny . . .'

'I . . . I . . .'

'Do you have to throw up? Because if you do I'm getting out of the way . . . I can't stand it when somebody throws up . . .'

'I'm not going to throw up!' Sally said.

'Then what?'

'I just got hot . . . that's all . . .' Sally mopped her forehead with the tails of her shirt.

'Well, don't fall off your bike,' Andrea said. 'You're riding so wobbly.'

'I won't.'

'Have a piece of candy . . . it'll make you feel better.'

'No! I already told you I wouldn't eat his candy . . . it could be poison.'

'Are you crazy?' Andrea said.

142

'No, I'm careful . . . and you should be too . . . I've never seen *him* eat his candy, have you?'

'How can he . . . he's got false teeth!' She crunched another piece of rock candy.

'You're going to ruin *your* teeth and wind up with false ones too!'

'Since when are you my mother?' Andrea asked.

The next morning at breakfast, Sally said, 'Whatever happened to Hitler?'

'Nobody's sure,' Douglas answered, his mouth full of cereal. 'Some people say he killed himself and others say he escaped to South America.'

'What do you think?' Sally asked Mom.

'I think he's dead.'

'He should be,' Ma Fanny said. 'If anybody deserves to be dead it's him.'

'I think he got away,' Douglas said. 'I'll bet he's in Argentina right now . . .'

'Or he could be here, in Miami Beach,' Sally said. 'I'll bet you never thought of that.'

Douglas coughed some cereal out of his mouth. 'Boy, are you a card.'

'What an idea,' Mom said. 'Hitler in Miami Beach . . .'

'God forbid,' Ma Fanny added.

Chapter 15

Dance ballerina, dance . . . Sally sang softly. She twirled around and around in her black inner tube, her head back, her eyes closed. The ocean was calm and blue and the sun hot on her face. Earlier, she had talked to Daddy on the phone. He had wished her a happy Hanukkah and said he'd be down to visit in just two more weeks. She wished he could be there tonight, to light the first candle on the menorah. It was hard to believe that Hanukkah was beginning. Usually the weather was very cold for her favourite holiday. Sometimes it even snowed. She laughed out loud at the idea of celebrating Hanukkah in the middle of summer, then opened her eyes to make sure no one had heard. It was okay. There was no one near enough to have noticed.

Dance ballerina, dance . . . what a good song! No wonder it was number one on the hit parade. After Christmas vacation she and Andrea were going to take ballet lessons. Their mothers had already signed them up at Miss Beverly's School of Classic Ballet. Sally could hardly wait. Her hands skimmed the water, keeping time to her music. She hoped that at Miss Beverly's ballet school she'd get to wear a tutu instead of an exercise dress. She pictured herself in pink net with pink satin toe slippers to match, like Margaret O'Brien in *The Unfinished Dance*, the best movie Sally had ever seen. Mom bought her the colouring book and the paper doll set because she'd enjoyed the film so much.

Some people, like Mrs Daniels from next door, thought fifth graders were too old for that stuff. Sally heard her say so to Mom. 'When my Bubbles was that age she was sewing her own clothes and reading fine literature from the library.' What Mrs Daniels didn't know was that you could play with paper dolls like a baby or you could play with them in a very grown-up way, making up stories inside your head. Like *Margaret O'Brien meets Mr Zavodsky . . .* This takes place before she becomes a famous movie star. She's just a regular kid, like Sally. Margaret finds out Mr Zavodsky is Adolf Hitler in disguise and reports him to the police. They capture Mr Zavodsky and award the Medal of Honour to Margaret O'Brien. At the medal ceremony a well-known Hollywood producer says, *We're looking for a girl just like you to play the lead in a new movie. How are you at ballet? Well, sir . . .* Margaret answers, *I'm in the Junior Advanced class and I hope to be in Advanced next year at the latest.* She then performs for him and gets the part.

It bothered Sally that Mom had said to Mrs Daniels, 'Each child matures at her own rate.' But Mom didn't know about Sally's stories, so maybe she thought Sally played like a baby too.

Suddenly Sally felt a sharp, stinging pain on her leg. She cried out and reached. Something was there. Something was on her leg. She tried to pull it off but the same pain hit her hand and wrist. 'Stop . . .'

145

she cried, 'stop it . . . stop it . . .' She began to kick and scream as the painful sting spread. She couldn't stop the stinging pain. 'Help . . .' she called. 'Please . . . somebody help me . . .'

It seemed like hours before the lifeguard reached her. He lifted her out of the tube, trying to hold her still, but the pain made her squirm and cry even though she knew it was important to be quiet during a rescue. She moaned and closed her eyes.

'You'll be okay now . . .' the lifeguard said. He sounded very far away. Sally wondered why. And then, everything went black.

When she opened her eyes again she was on the beach, wrapped in a blanket, and Mom was at her side. She could hear Ma Fanny and Douglas talking to her, but she couldn't turn her head to see them. A crowd had gathered around her. 'Oh, my baby . . . my poor little girl . . .' Mom cried.

'It hurts,' Sally said. She closed her eyes again, too tired to say any more.

'How could such a thing have happened?' she heard her mother ask, and was surprised that Mom sounded so angry.

'I don't know, Ma'am . . .' the lifeguard answered. 'We had no warning . . . you can look through my glasses yourself . . . there's not another Man O'War in sight.'

'Are you absolutely sure that's what it was?' Mom asked.

'Yes, Ma'am . . . positive . . . wrapped itself right around her leg and when she tried to pull it off it got her hand. I've seen plenty of cases and it hurts like hell . . . pardon my language . . . but she'll be okay. You can call the Board of Health . . . they'll tell you what to do.'

'Come . . .' Ma Fanny said, 'let's get her home.'

'But how?' Mom sounded confused now and frightened. 'She can't walk . . .'

'Never mind,' Ma Fanny said. 'Dougie . . . go and ask that woman if we can borrow her baby stroller . . . tell her we'll bring it back right away.'

'For Sally?' Douglas asked.

Sally tried to open her eyes again, tried to speak, but she hadn't the strength. The pain was less acute now but she could still feel the stinging and she couldn't move her fingers or toes.

'Just go and do it, Douglas!' Mom said.

'Okay . . . but Sally won't like it.'

'Never mind,' Mom said. 'She'll never know . . . she's only half-conscious . . . you can see that . . .'

I am not, Sally wanted to say. I can hear every word and I'll die if you take me home like a baby!

'I'll carry her for you, Ma'am,' the lifeguard said and Sally felt his arms around her again.

He lowered her into the stroller. Sally kept her eyes tightly shut. If any of her friends were around she didn't want to know.

'Watch her legs,' Mom said. 'Let them dangle over the sides . . . that's it.'

'Can you make it home now, Ma'am?' the lifeguard asked.

'Yes, I think so . . . and thank you very much.'

147

'Any time.'

'I'll push her,' Douglas said.

'No,' Mom told him, 'I will. You walk at her side and make sure she doesn't fall out.'

Sally felt herself moving, first on grass and then on concrete. 'Listen, Ma . . .' Mom said to Ma Fanny, 'you better walk home slowly. I don't want you to get out of breath and have a spell.'

'Spell . . . schmell . . .' Ma Fanny said. 'I can keep up with anybody.'

The Board of Health told Mom that Sally should sit in a tub of tepid water with baking soda. She soaked so long, the skin on her fingers and toes got crinkly. The pain eased up and soon she could move her fingers again. The family took turns sitting in the bathroom with her. She didn't mind because she was still wearing her bathing suit. Besides, she was grateful for the company. She watched as Mom filed her nails, as Ma Fanny worked on her afghan, and as Douglas blew the insides out of an egg.

'You were pretty brave,' Douglas said, pausing for a breath. 'You really surprised me.'

'I screamed in the water,' Sally said. 'I remember . . .'

'Yeah . . . but once you were on the beach you shut up.'

'Because it hurt too bad to do anything,' Sally said.

'Worse than a shot?'

'Much worse.'

'Worse than a bee sting?'

'I don't know . . . I never got stung by a bee . . . but Christine did once, on the bottom of her foot. She cried a lot.'

'She would!' Douglas held his eggshell up to the light. 'I wonder if it hurt worse than my kidney infection?'

'I can't say . . . I've never had a kidney infection.'

'It looked like it hurt worse.'

Sally shrugged.

'I hope I never get stung by a Man O'War,' Douglas said.

'I hope you don't either . . . I wouldn't wish that on anybody . . . not even Harriet Goodman and I hate her.'

'Who's Harriet Goodman?'

'This jerk in my class who hates me for no reason.'

'Oh.'

Three hours later Mom said, 'Okay . . . you can get out now.'

Sally pulled the stopper from the tub. 'At last!'

'I'll help you,' Mom said. 'I don't want you to faint again.'

'Is that what happened before . . . when everything got black?'

'Yes, you passed out . . . and the lifeguard said it's lucky you did . . . because you were fighting him so badly he could hardly handle you.'

At sundown they lit the first candle on the menorah and sang the Hanukkah blessing. Sally was lying on the sofa with a thick, baking soda paste covering her hand and leg, where she'd been stung. It felt yuckiest between her toes.

All the neighbours came to visit that night.

Andrea said, 'Of all days to go to Monkey Jungle . . . and just when something exciting happened . . .'

'How was it?' Sally asked.

'To tell the truth, it wasn't that great . . . and you could smell monkeys everywhere.'

'My mother thinks you can get diseases from monkeys so I'll probably never get there,' Sally said.

'Well, you're not missing much.'

'But I like chimps . . .'

'So do I . . . but not *that* many at one time . . . besides, I'd have rather been at the beach with you.'

'Then you might have been stung by a Man O'War too.'

'I know . . .'

'And it wasn't any fun . . . I'll tell you that . . .'

'So I hear . . .'

'But Douglas says I was really brave.'

'Brave is a matter of opinion,' Andrea said. 'Everyone acts differently in an emergency . . . passing out isn't necessarily brave.'

'I didn't *want* to pass out . . . it just happened.'

'Don't get me wrong . . . I'm not saying it *wasn't* brave to pass out . . . who knows, I might have done the same thing.' She looked down for a minute. 'Anyway, I'm glad you're okay now.'

'Thanks.'

Mrs Daniels came over with a honey cake. 'My

Bubbles was stung two years ago . . . on her foot . . . we went straight to the hospital . . . when it comes to my Bubbles we don't fool around.'

'We don't fool around when it comes to our children either,' Mom said. 'When Douglas had nephritis we went to the biggest specialist in New Jersey. And today, we called the Board of Health about Sally.'

'The Board of Health!' Mrs Daniels said. 'Who'd trust them?'

'What did they do for Bubbles in the hospital?' Mom asked.

'Told us to put her in a tub of baking-soda water.'

'Well, that's exactly what the Board of Health told us.' Sally could tell that Mom was pleased. 'And now she's just fine, as you can see for yourself.'

'So this time you were lucky,' Mrs Daniels said.

'Knock wood!' Ma Fanny thumped the dining table.

'Knock wood,' Mrs Daniels repeated.

Later, before she went to sleep, Douglas gave Sally a freshly painted egg shell. 'It's supposed to be Margaret O'Brien.'

Sally held the fragile shell in the palm of her good hand. 'I can tell by the braids,' she said. 'It's a beautiful shell . . . the best one you've ever done.'

Douglas half-smiled. 'It'll stand by itself on your shelf . . . the feet are supposed to be ballet shoes but I had to make them kind of wide to support the weight . . . so they might not look like ballet shoes to you . . .'

151

'Oh, no . . .' Sally said. 'I can tell they are . . .'

'Good.'

'Thank you, Douglas.'

'Goodnight . . . I'm glad you're okay,' Douglas said.

Chapter 16

'No school for you today!' Mom said the next morning.

'But I'm fine,' Sally told her.

'We're not going to take any chances. A day of rest can't hurt.'

'But I don't want to miss school today . . . we're having a Hanukkah party with songs and games . . .'

'I know, honey . . . but your health comes first,' Mom said.

'Please, Mom . . . please let me go to school . . .'

'We'll have our own Hanukkah party, right here,' Mom said.

'That's not the same!'

'Tell you what . . . I was saving your Hanukkah present until Daddy gets here, but I'm sure he'll understand if I give it to you now . . .'

'My Hanukkah present?' Can it be a baton? she wondered.

Mom went into the sleeping alcove and came back with a slender box. 'I haven't even wrapped it yet.'

It can't be a baton, Sally thought, opening the box. It's much too small. Instead, she found a Mickey Mouse watch with a red patent leather strap. 'Oh, Mom . . . I love it! It's exactly what I wanted. It's even better than a baton. Oh, thank you . . . thank you . . .' She jumped off the day bed and hugged her mother.

'I didn't know you wanted a baton,' Mom said.

'You didn't?'

'No . . . you never mentioned it.'

'You mean I forgot? Oh well . . . it doesn't matter . . . because this is even better . . . and now I've just *got* to go to school . . . I've got to show all my friends my new watch.'

'Tomorrow . . .' Mom said, laughing. 'Today you stay on your bed and rest.'

So Sally rested. She watched the hours go by on her new watch. She read a Nancy Drew mystery. She studied Ma Fanny's collection of family photos. She always had trouble believing that the chubby baby on Ma Fanny's lap was once her mother. And then there was her favourite picture. Lila. She held it, running her hands along the silver frame, then tracing Lila's features with one finger – her eyes, nose, mouth – beautiful Lila.

Dear Mr Zavodsky,
I'm thinking about you. I know you didn't get my
other letters because I didn't send them yet. But
that doesn't mean I'm not going to send them
because I am. They are safe, inside my keepsake
box. I am just waiting for the right moment. A
detective has to get evidence and that is what I'm
doing now. I know plenty about you. I know you
killed Lila. So don't think that just because
you haven't heard from me you're safe.

Two weeks later, when Sally's father arrived, they joined the Seagull Pool Club. Mom said it had nothing to do with the Man O'Wars in the ocean but Sally didn't believe her.

'Does this mean we can't go to the beach any more?' she asked.

'Of course not,' Daddy said. 'This is just something extra.'

'And you can take swimming lessons,' Mom said. 'I hear they have an excellent instructor.'

'I can already float on my back.'

'But there are lots of other strokes,' Daddy said.

'I don't want swimming lessons. I'd rather learn by myself,' Sally said.

'Well, that's all right too,' Mom told her. 'You know I don't believe in forcing children when it comes to swimming.'

'And neither do I,' Daddy added.

'I'm hoping Douglas will make some friends at the pool,' Mom said, more to Daddy than Sally. 'He's always alone, riding his bicycle . . . even on the beach he keeps to himself . . .'

'Douglas doesn't need friends,' Sally said.

'Everybody needs friends,' Mom said. 'Even Douglas.'

It wasn't that Sally objected to joining the Seagull Pool Club. Shelby belonged there and so did a lot of other kids from school. It was just that she wanted to make sure she could still go to the beach. In spite of the Man O' Wars, she loved the ocean – the smell of it, the sound of it, the salty taste – her toes squishing into the sand at the water's edge . . .

★

On her first day at the Seagull Pool Club, Shelby taught Sally how to hold her nose and sit on the bottom. Then Sally showed Shelby how she could float on her back. While she was demonstrating, someone swam so close she felt a foot brush the side of her face. 'Hey . . .' Sally called, losing her balance. She stood in waist-high water. 'Why don't you watch where you're going?'

He turned to face her. 'Why don't you watch out yourself?' he drawled. It was Georgia Blue Eyes.

'Did you see that boy who kicked me?' Sally asked Shelby.

'Yes.'

'Well, Andrea is hopelessly in love with him.'

'She is?'

'Oops . . .' Sally covered her mouth with her hand. 'That's supposed to be a secret. I shouldn't have told you.'

'It's okay,' Shelby said. 'I know how to keep secrets.'

'How was the Seagull?' Andrea asked that night. They were sitting at the side of the goldfish pool, watching Omar stalk a salamander.

'It was pretty good,' Sally said, stirring the fish pool with a long stick.

'Any interesting boys?'

'I haven't looked around yet.' Sally was surprised by her own answer. She had expected to tell Andrea about Georgia Blue Eyes right away. But having a secret from Andrea was so exciting she decided to keep her news to herself. Someday she would tell Andrea. Some day when the time was right. She would say, *Oh, by the way . . . Georgia Blue Eyes once put his foot in my face.*

'We might join in March,' Andrea said. 'My father's going to think about it. He got me and Linda a raft for Hanukkah . . . we rode the waves all day . . . it was so much fun.'

'Shelby taught me to hold my nose and sit on the bottom of the pool.'

'I don't like water in my eyes.'

'Me neither . . . but Shelby told me to keep them closed and I wouldn't feel a thing.'

'Yes . . . but you could bump into someone that way.'

'Listen,' Sally said, 'you could bump into someone just floating on your back . . . you never know . . .'

'That's true,' Andrea said.

'I don't want to fly to Cuba,' Mom said.

'Just for the weekend, Louise,' Daddy told her.

Sally sat at the table in the breakfast nook, shelling lima beans for Ma Fanny, who was in the kitchen, fixing dinner. She and Ma Fanny were very quiet so that they could hear the conversation between Daddy and Mom, who were in the sleeping alcove.

'No . . . I don't want to go, Arnold.'

'Because of Vicki and Ted?'

'Because I'm afraid to fly . . . and you know it.'

'Is that the whole reason?' Daddy asked.

'It's reason enough.'

'There's nothing to be afraid of . . . I've flown three times since you've been down here . . .'

'And I wish to God you wouldn't . . . I wish you'd take the train down and back.'

Sally nodded. She worried so each time her father flew.

'I'd lose two days that way,' Daddy said.

'But at least you'd be safe,' Mom told him.

Sally nodded again.

'If your time's up, it's up . . . it doesn't matter where you are,' Daddy said.

'You don't have to take chances though . . . you don't have to go looking for trouble.'

'That's right,' Sally mumbled to herself. 'Especially this year.' She finished shelling the beans. She dumped them out on the table and began dividing them into five equal piles.

'I want to go to Cuba for the weekend.' Daddy sounded very firm. 'And I want you to come with me.'

'No!' Mom said, sounding just as firm.

'I'm going, Lou . . . with you or without you.'

'Then I guess you don't love me very much.' Mom's voice broke.

Sally paused, feeling herself choke up.

'This has nothing to do with love,' Daddy said, quietly.

'It has everything to do with love.' Mom was crying now.

'If you loved me *enough* you'd come too,' Daddy said.

Sally was afraid to look up from the table. She didn't want to meet Ma Fanny's glance.

'You only want to go because of Ted and Vicki . . . they put the bug in your head . . .'

Daddy sighed, 'Oh, Lou . . . why can't you understand . . . I need to get away with *you* . . . I need that badly . . .'

'I need it too,' Mom said, sniffling. 'But I'd rather move up to a hotel on Lincoln Road. Why do we have to fly to Cuba?'

'Because Ted will pick up the tab, for one thing . . . and for another, it's an adventure . . .'

'I'm not Sally,' Mom said. 'You can't convince me by calling this an adventure!'

Sally sat up straight.

'Shush . . . she'll hear you.'

'I don't care!'

'Maybe you should be more like Sally,' Daddy said. 'At least she's willing to try.'

Sally couldn't help smiling.

'You're ruining our time together, Arnold . . . I don't understand why you're doing this to us.'

'Why *I'm* doing it!' Daddy said. 'Okay . . . not another word on the subject . . . but next Friday night I'm flying to Cuba with Ted and Vicki. I'll have two tickets in my pocket. I hope you'll change your mind and come with us.'

Daddy clumped out of the sleeping alcove, still wearing his wooden beach shoes. Sally pretended to be busy with the lima beans as he walked over to her.

He put his hand on her head. 'How's my little gal?' he asked.

'Oh . . . just fine,' Sally told him.

'Good . . . that's good . . .'

'We each get twenty-six lima beans for supper.'

'Suppose I eat twenty-seven?' Daddy asked.

'Then we'll all point and call *pig* . . .'

Daddy laughed and took a lima bean from one of the carefully arranged piles. He ate it raw.

The next morning Sally went grocery shopping with Mom and Ma Fanny. She needed a new box of Crayolas and she also wanted to make sure Mom bought enough Welch's grape juice.

'Get smart, Louise,' Ma Fanny said. 'Go to Cuba for the weekend. There's nothing to worry about here.'

'I don't know, Ma . . . both of us on the same plane . . . if anything happens what will become of the children?'

'Nothing will happen.'

'You can't be sure.'

'So who's ever sure of anything in this crazy world? Go with Arnold . . . don't send him away without you.'

'I'll think about it, Ma.' Mom looked over at Sally. 'Don't you know better than to listen to grown-ups when they're talking?'

'I wasn't listening,' Sally said. 'I don't care if you go to Cuba or not.' She pushed her cart down the aisle. Actually, Sally was torn between wanting Mom

160

to go because Daddy seemed so anxious and wanting them both to stay home. After all, it would be more than a month before she'd see her father again. It bothered her that he wanted to get away with just Mom.

Sally and her family went to the Seagull Pool Club every day that week. It was such fun to have Daddy with them! He never tired of playing games. He played dolphin with Sally, letting her ride on his back as he swam underwater. He lifted her on to his shoulders and had chicken fights with Douglas, who carried Shelby as his partner. He played keep-away, tossing a brightly coloured beach ball from one to the other. He rented flippers for their feet, showing them how to use them. And suddenly, to Sally's surprise, she found that she could lift both feet off the bottom of the pool and not go under. She was learning to swim! It was easy. All she had to do was kick her feet and move her arms. She was actually *swimming* and without ever having had a lesson!

Mom stood at the edge of the pool snapping pictures.

On Thursday, Sally brought Barbara as her guest. 'Barbara . . . you know Shelby, don't you?' she said, when they met in the pool.

'Oh, sure . . .' Barbara said. 'You're the other one who's allergic to the school food, right?'

'Right!' Shelby answered and all three of them laughed together.

That afternoon Sally spoke to Georgia Blue Eyes.

She said, 'You know something . . . you're a good swimmer but you're always bumping into me when I'm floating on my back.'

He said, 'If you'd turn over once in a while you wouldn't have that problem.'

She said, 'You're the one with the problem.'

He said, 'I've seen you around, haven't I?'

She said, 'Maybe . . .'

He said, 'You're always with that other one . . . that jerk with the frizzy hair.'

She said, 'Her name is Andrea and her hair's not frizzy . . . it's curly.'

He said, 'And what's your name?'

She said, 'Mine?' and she looked over at Shelby and Barbara who were giggling like crazy. 'I'm Sally.'

'Sally what?' he asked.

'Never mind,' Sally said.

'Sally Nevermind . . . that's a pretty jerky name . . . but it fits you . . .' He laughed and swam away.

'Oh . . . he's so cute!' Barbara said. 'Don't you think he's the most adorable boy you've ever seen?'

'Yes,' Shelby said. 'And I love his accent . . . I'd let him kiss me any day.'

'Me too,' Barbara said. 'Any day and any place.'

'What about you, Sally?' Shelby asked. 'Would you let him kiss you?'

'I'd have to think about it,' Sally answered. 'I usually prefer Latin lovers . . . they're the best.'

On Saturday afternoon Sally and Douglas went to the beach with Ma Fanny and the Rubins. There

162

were no Man O'Wars in sight. Mrs Rubin sat on her blanket rubbing suntan oil on to Mr Rubin's back. 'Your mother's so lucky . . .' she said to Sally. 'Going off to Cuba for the weekend . . . I wish somebody would take me to Cuba . . . hint, hint . . .' She tickled Mr Rubin's belly.

He said, 'Somebody's already paying to keep you in Miami Beach . . . remember?'

'Oh, Ivan . . . I was just teasing,' Mrs Rubin said. 'You know that.' She kissed his cheek.

'My mother didn't even want to go,' Sally explained. 'My father practically had to force her . . .'

'Sally,' Ma Fanny called, 'come and have a sandwich.'

'I'm not hungry yet.'

'Come and have it anyway . . .' Ma Fanny said.

When Sally sat down next to her, Ma Fanny leaned close and whispered, 'Don't tell family secrets.'

'But I . . .'

'Think, mumeshana . . . always think before you speak.'

'I try to . . .' Sally said.

'I loved it, I loved it, I loved it!' Mom sang, when she and Daddy returned from Cuba on Sunday night. 'It was even more exciting than Daddy promised.'

'Did you see any Latin lovers?' Sally asked.

'Oh, dozens . . . everywhere you looked . . .' She and Daddy laughed. 'And we rhumbaed until three in the morning . . .' She put her arms around Daddy's neck and they danced across the room. 'And we

drank Crème de Cacao . . . and it was so delicious . . .'

'As good as champagne?' Sally asked.

'Oh, better . . . much, much better . . .' Mom
laughed some more. 'It makes you feel like you're
walking on air.'

'And what about flying?' Sally said. 'How was
that?'

'Well . . .' Mom answered, 'once we got up I never
even knew we were moving . . .'

'Once she opened her eyes, that is,' Daddy said,
'*and* stopped digging her nails into my hand . . .'

'Oh, Arnold . . .' Mom gave him a playful punch.
'Not that I'd want to do it all the time, mind you . . .
but once in a while . . . in good weather . . .'

Sally noticed that her parents looked at each other
and laughed a lot in the next few days. On New
Year's Eve they all went to the Orange Bowl Parade.
Mr Wiskoff had a box, right up front, so Sally had
no trouble seeing all the marching bands and floats
go by. And after the parade Big Ted took Sally by
the hand, to his car, and gave her a special gift – a
baton. 'Someday we're going to see *you* march in the
Orange Bowl Parade,' he said.

'But how did you know . . .' Sally asked, 'how did
you know I've been dying for a baton?'

'A little bird told me,' he said.

And then it was January second and Daddy had to
fly back to New Jersey. They went to the airport

164

to see him off. Sally waved and blew kisses and prayed hard as the plane took off.

And then it was January third and time to go back to school.

Chapter 17

Sally couldn't find her library book. 'It's due today,' she said. 'I can't go to school without it.'

'Did you look under the day bed?' Mom asked.

'I've looked everywhere . . .' Sally picked at her cuticles. 'I'm going to be late.' If you were late to Central Beach Elementary School you had to go to the Vice-Principal's office for a late slip and Sally had heard that the Vice-Principal was so mean three kids had fainted and two had thrown up just from being late to school last month.

'Think . . .' Ma Fanny said. 'Where was the last place you saw it?'

'I don't remember . . . in the kitchen, maybe . . . before Daddy came.'

Ma Fanny walked away. In a few minutes she came back with Sally's book. 'So . . .' she said, handing it to Sally.

'You found it!' Sally had searched so carefully she couldn't believe it. 'Where . . . where was it?'

'In the pantry,' Ma Fanny said, as if that were the logical place for a book to be.

'How did it get in there?' Mom asked.

Sally raised her shoulders and held up her hands. She and her mother looked at Ma Fanny.

'So what's wrong with reading a book in English now and then?' Ma Fanny said. 'How is a person supposed to learn if she doesn't practise?' She kissed

Sally's forehead. 'Hurry to school now, sweetie pie . . .'

Sally ran all the way but the second bell rang just as she reached her corridor. She knew the rules. She was supposed to go straight to the office. But maybe she could sneak into her classroom. Maybe Miss Swetnick wouldn't notice. Of course, if they'd already started opening exercises she'd have no choice. She'd have to go to the office. And she'd eaten scrambled eggs for breakfast. Just the thought of throwing them up in front of the Vice-Principal was enough to make her feel sick. Maybe she'd get lucky. Maybe she'd faint instead.

She stood outside her classroom. It was very noisy. They weren't having opening exercises yet. Miss Swetnick was standing at the front of the room waving her hand around. She noticed Sally, standing in the doorway.

Sally felt her stomach roll over. Now she would be sent to the Vice-Principal.

'Well . . . good morning, Sally.'

'Good morning,' Sally said. 'I'm late . . .'

'So I see,' Miss Swetnick said. She was wearing her pale blue blouse and her hair was tied back with the same colour ribbon.

Sally didn't move.

'Well . . . don't just stand there . . . come in and take your seat,' Miss Swetnick said.

'But I'm late.'

'You've already said that . . . but this is the first time you've been late, isn't it?'

'Yes.'

'And I'm sure you've a good reason . . .'

'Oh, I do . . . my library book is due today and I couldn't find it . . .'

'You see . . .' Miss Swetnick said.

'Then I don't have to go to the office?'

'Not this time.'

Sally thought, Miss Swetnick is the nicest, most fair teacher in the whole world. And also, the prettiest.

'Besides,' Miss Swetnick said, 'today is a special day . . . I've just told the class I'm engaged to be married.' She smiled and held out her hand, showing Sally a gold ring with a tiny diamond in the centre.

'Congratulations!' Sally said, wondering if Miss Swetnick knew how to wash diamonds. She took her seat.

'Now . . . let's get on with our geography,' Miss Swetnick said. 'Page eighty-seven . . . Harriet, would you begin, please.'

Peter leaned close to Sally and whispered, 'She's marrying my brother!' Before Sally had a chance to answer him, Harriet called out, 'When's the wedding, Miss Swetnick?'

'We're doing geography now, Harriet . . .'

'But you haven't told us when you're getting married.'

'Over Easter vacation,' Miss Swetnick said. 'Please begin with the first paragraph, Harriet . . .'

'But you'll still be our teacher, won't you?' Harriet asked.

'Yes, of course.'

'Where are you going on your honeymoon?'

'Harriet . . . we're doing our geography now,' Miss Swetnick said.

'But that *is* geography . . . you're going *some place*, aren't you?'

'Yes, we're going to Cuba. Now that's the last question I'm going to answer . . . so please begin, Harriet.'

'Okay,' Harriet said, opening her book. 'Florida is a land of great beauty . . .'

During recess Peter Hornstein said, 'It sure is great to have your sister-in-law for a teacher.'

'She's not your sister-in-law yet,' Harriet reminded him.

'Yeah . . . but she can't keep her *almost* brother-in-law after school . . . how would that look?'

'Miss Swetnick is very fair,' Sally said. 'She doesn't play favourites.'

'Just because she didn't send you to the office this morning . . . that doesn't mean anything.'

'We'll see,' Sally said.

'We sure will,' Peter told her.

That afternoon, during a spelling bee, Sally missed the word *Pacific* on the fourth round and had to take her seat. Peter had missed on the second round so he was seated too. As soon as she felt the tug on her braid Sally knew that Peter was about to dip her hair in his inkwell, but this time she didn't have to say anything because Miss Swetnick saw the whole thing.

'Peter Hornstein! How many times have I told you to keep your hands off Sally's hair? Three days after school and thirty *I will nots* in your notebook.'

'But Miss Swetnick . . .' Peter began.

'You know better, Peter.'

'But Miss Swetnick . . .'

'Did you think I wouldn't keep you after school just because we're practically related?'

'No, Ma'am . . . I never thought that.'

'I'm glad . . . now, let's get back to our spelling bee. Barbara, can you spell the word, *university*. . . .'

'U-n-i-v-e-r-s-i-t-y.' Barbara won the spelling bee. She won almost every week. She would certainly be the class representative to the school spelling bee and if she won that she'd go to the county spelling bee and if she won that she'd go to the state spelling bee and get her picture in the newspapers. Sally wished she could spell the same way Barbara could. Or was it just that Miss Swetnick gave Sally harder words? No, she wouldn't do that . . . after all, she was a very fair teacher.

'Who's that fat girl with Douglas?' Barbara asked Sally. They were taking a short cut to Barbara's house, after school, across the grounds of Miami Beach Junior-Senior High.

'Where?' Sally asked.

'Over there . . . see . . .' Barbara pointed to a palm tree.

'I don't know,' Sally said, spotting them on the grass. 'I've never seen her before.'

'Probably his girlfriend,' Barbara said.

'No . . . Douglas doesn't have any friends.'

'Everybody has friends.'

'Not Douglas . . . he's different,' Sally said. 'He had two in New Jersey but he doesn't have any here.'

'I'll bet he does,' Barbara said, 'and that he just doesn't tell you about them.'

'Douglas doesn't tell us about anything!'

'You see . . .' Barbara said.

When Douglas came home for supper, Sally was outside, waiting for him. 'Who was that girl?' she asked.

'What girl?'

'Under the tree . . . this afternoon . . . I saw you . . .'

'Oh, that girl . . . that was Darlene.'

'Who's Darlene?' Sally said.

'The girl under the tree.'

'I mean *who* is she?'

'A friend . . . why?' Douglas asked.

So, Barbara was right after all, Sally thought. 'How do you know her?'

'From school . . . what is this . . . twenty questions?'

'I'm just curious . . . does she live around here?'

'No, she lives on an island in Biscayne Bay.'

'Isn't that where the millionaires live?' Sally asked.

'Yeah . . .'

'Is she a millionaire?'

'You know something, Sally . . . you're starting to sound just like Mom!'

'I am not . . . I just want to know what's going on for a change!'

Sally sat down at the table in the dining alcove. Aunt Bette had sent her a new box of stationery. *Sayings From Sally* was printed across the top of every sheet. She wrote a short thank you note to Aunt Bette, then put the box back on her shelf and took a piece of paper from her old Bambi stationery.

She couldn't write to *him* on name paper.

Dear Mr Zavodsky,
You haven't seen me around much lately because I've been very busy. But that doesn't mean I don't know what's going on. I'm still on your case even when I don't see you. So don't get any wrong ideas and think you're home free.

The next day Sally went to Barbara's house again. They were going to practise twirling batons. 'You were right,' Sally said. 'Douglas does have a friend. Her name's Darlene.'

'You see . . .' Barbara said, 'I told you so.'

'She lives on an island in Biscayne Bay.'

'Oh . . . one of those!'

'Douglas wouldn't tell me anything else about her.'

'I'll get Marla to find out for us,' Barbara said. They practised twirling in Barbara's front yard. Barbara was getting very good. She could toss her baton into the air and catch it as it came down without missing a beat. Sally hadn't mastered that trick yet. She always closed her eyes at the last

172

moment, sure the baton would hit her in the head, and usually it did. But she could twirl it under her leg and switch hands.

'I want to twirl in the Orange Bowl parade next New Year's Eve,' Barbara said.

'Oh, me too,' Sally said, and she marched across the yard with her knees high and her head back. 'How do I look?'

'A lot better,' Barbara said, as Sally strutted in front of her. 'I hope I get to wear the same uniform as my sister . . . I love her white boots and her red dress.'

'I like her hat best,' Sally said, 'with all that gold braid.'

Barbara did her figure eights so fast her baton looked like it had a motor.

'We could march together in the parade,' Sally said tentatively, not sure if Barbara considered her an equal in twirling.

'Yes . . . and be the first and only Central Beach kids *ever* in the parade.'

Sally felt more sure of herself then. 'They'll announce the debut of Barbara Ash and Sally Freedman and we'll march in front of the best float like this . . . *dum dum dee dah dah* . . .' she sang as she strutted across the yard.

'Did you hear where Miss Swetnick's going on her honeymoon?' Barbara asked, tossing her baton into the air.

'Yes, to Cuba.'

'Isn't that a dumb place to go for a honeymoon?'

'I don't know . . . my parents were there over Christmas vacation and they said it was great.'

'If you like cigars . . .'

Sally laughed. 'My parents don't like cigars . . . especially my mother.'

'But that's what Cuba's famous for.'

'That's not the only thing,' Sally said. 'They have this drink called Creme de Cacao that's supposed to be really something . . . it makes you feel like you're walking on air . . .'

'I've never heard of it.'

'My mother told me . . .'

Barbara sank to her knees, whipping her baton from hand to hand. 'We've got cocoa and cream . . . we could make some . . .'

'It's got something else in it too,' Sally said. 'Some kind of whisky, I think.'

'We've got whisky,' Barbara said. 'And I'm getting thirsty . . .'

They went inside, to the kitchen, where Barbara gathered the ingredients. She mixed the cocoa and cream, then added a dash of whisky.

'Are you allowed to drink that?' Sally asked, eyeing the whisky bottle. It was called Johnnie Walker.

'I've never asked,' Barbara said, stirring in some sugar. 'This is instant cocoa . . . we don't need to heat it.' She handed Sally a cup. 'Well . . . here's looking at you,' she said, clinking cups with Sally.

Sally took a sip, then waited for Barbara to do the same.

'What do you think?' Barbara asked.

'Not bad,' Sally said, afraid of hurting Barbara's feelings.

'I don't like it,' Barbara said, wiping her mouth with the back of her hand. 'It doesn't make me feel like I'm walking on air . . .'

'Me neither,' Sally said.

'Let's have grape juice instead.' Barbara rinsed out their cups and poured the grape juice.

'It might have tasted good without the whisky,' Sally said.

'But then it would have been just plain cocoa.'

'I suppose you're right.'

'I could tell you a secret about whisky,' Barbara said.

'Tell me . . .'

'Only if you promise never to breathe a word . . .'

'I promise . . .'

'Swear it?'

'I swear . . .'

'Every Saturday night my mother gets drunk.' Barbara took a long drink of juice.

'She does?' Sally asked.

'Yes . . . she drinks until she passes out. She listens to records . . . the ones she and my father used to play . . . and she gets out the old scrap-books . . . and she cries and she drinks . . . she thinks me and Marla don't know because she gives us money for the movies . . . to get us out of the house . . . but we know . . . and on Sundays she says she thinks she's catching cold and she stays in bed all day . . . she doesn't touch a drop the rest of the week though . . .'

'That's sad . . .' Sally didn't know what else to say.

'Yes . . . it would be better if she'd come out and tell us how she's feeling . . .'

'Grown-ups always keep things to themselves, don't they?' Sally said.

'They seem to.'

'But it's better to share your problems with a friend, don't you think?'

'Well . . . I feel better since I told you about my mother,' Barbara said, quietly.

Sally looked away for a moment, then said, 'I've got a secret too . . .'

'About your mother?'

'No . . . my father.'

'He drinks?'

'No . . .'

'Well what is it?'

'Cross your heart and hope to die you'll never tell?'

'Cross my heart . . .'

'I've never told anyone about this . . .' Sally said, reconsidering.

'You'll feel better when you do,' Barbara told her.

'Okay . . . I'm scared my father's going to die this year.'

'Why, is he sick?'

'No . . . but both his brothers died when they were forty-two and that's how old my father is.'

'Were they sick first?' Barbara asked, pouring more juice.

'One was and the other wasn't . . . he just dropped dead.'

'That's pretty scary,' Barbara said.

'I know . . . I pray for him every night.'

'I prayed for my father during the war . . .'

'But you were just a little kid then.'

'So? I prayed with my mother and Marla every single night . . . but it didn't do any good.'

Chapter 18

Sally caught Virus X. It was going around. Her head hurt and she felt weak and dizzy when she tried to stand. Ma Fanny sat beside her and showed her a story in *The Forward*. 'You see . . .' she said, tapping her paper, 'all the famous people in Hollywood have Virus X too. You're right in style.'

'I don't feel in style.'

'Three days and you'll be better. It says so right here.' She began to read. 'Virus X strikes movie stars, Esther Williams and Margaret O'Brien . . .'

'Where . . . where does it say that?' Sally asked, sitting up. 'Show me those names.'

Ma Fanny laughed. 'Okay . . . so maybe not both of your favourites at once but a lot of famous people just the same.'

'Famous schmamous,' Sally said, imitating Ma Fanny. She rolled over in her bed and moaned, 'I'm not *longed* for this world . . .'

Dr Spear came to the house to examine Sally. 'You'll be just fine,' he said, handing her a lollipop from his black bag.

'What about medicine?' Mom asked.

'None needed . . . three days and she'll be as good as new.'

'I told you,' Ma Fanny said. 'I read it in my paper.'

Mom ignored Ma Fanny's remark and asked the doctor, 'What about Douglas . . . it could be dangerous for him to come into contact with Sally's germs . . . should I send him to stay with friends until she's well?'

'I wouldn't bother,' Dr Spear said. 'Virus X is a relatively mild bug . . . and even if Douglas comes down with it there's not much we can do . . . let's just wait . . . no need to worry in advance.'

'Easier said than done,' Mom told him.

'Look, Mrs Freedman . . . all of Douglas's blood tests have been normal. You really have two fine, healthy children . . .' He looked over at Sally and winked. 'So why do you worry so?'

'It's my nature,' Mom said.

'Try to relax . . . I can prescribe something to help if you like . . .'

'No, no . . . I don't need anything. I just want my children to stay healthy . . . that's all I ask.'

'Take each day as it comes,' Dr Spear advised.

'I'll try,' Mom said. 'And thanks for coming . . . I know how busy you are.'

Later when Ma Fanny went to the kitchen to make a fresh orangeade for Sally, she said, 'Maybe the doctor's right, Louise. You should try to relax more.'

'I play mah-jong twice a week,' Mom said.

'But the rest of the time you sit home and read . . . you'll ruin your eyes.'

'My eyes are fine.'

'Maybe you should get out more with people . . . not just me and the women in this house . . . they could drive anybody crazy . . . one, two, three . . .'

179

'Look, Ma . . . I enjoy Eileen's company . . . she's a very good friend to me down here . . . and other than that I'm busy with the children . . . they're my life.'

'And mine too, you please shouldn't forget,' Ma Fanny said.

On Sally's third day home from school Andrea woke up with Virus X too and Mrs Rubin was so concerned about Linda she sent her to stay at the Shelbourne Hotel with her grandmother. Sally thought Linda was very lucky because the Shelbourne Hotel was one of the prettiest on Collins Avenue.

Ma Fanny made chicken soup with rice for Sally's lunch. It was the first time Sally had felt hungry since coming down with Virus X. While she was having her second bowl, the doorbell rang. It was the man from the telephone company, ready to install their phone.

'At last!' Mom said. 'I'd just about given up hope.'

'You and everybody else,' the telephone man said. He had a toothpick in his mouth and when he spoke he kept his teeth together so that he sounded like Humphrey Bogart, the movie star.

'Now we'll be able to talk to Daddy without the whole world listening,' Mom told Sally.

'And I won't have to stand on a chair to reach *this* phone,' Sally said.

'That's right.' Mom smiled and ran her fingers through Sally's hair.

When he'd finished, the telephone man said, 'Okay . . . this is a four-party line so when you . . .'

Mom interrupted him. 'But we requested a private line . . . we've always had a private line . . .'

'Listen, lady . . . you're lucky to be getting any kind of line . . . we have a long list of people who'd be happy with this set-up.'

'It's not that I'm unhappy,' Mom said, 'it's just that I thought . . .'

'It won't be as bad as it sounds,' the telephone man said. 'You'll get used to it.' He took the toothpick out of his mouth and put it in the ashtray. 'Okay . . .' he said, opening and closing his mouth a few times, as if he were testing his jaw to make sure it worked. 'Your signal is one long ring, followed by two short ones.'

'What do you mean?' Sally asked.

'It'll sound like this,' he said, 'brrriiinngg . . . brring, brring . . .'

Sally laughed. 'What a funny telephone!'

'It may be funny, sister, but it works!'

'What will the other signals sound like?' Sally asked.

'The only one you need to worry about is your own,' he said. 'I don't have time for long demonstrations. I've got to hook up your neighbours too.'

'The Rubins?' Sally asked.

The telephone man checked his book. 'No . . . the Daniels.'

'Oh, them . . .' Sally said. 'That should make Bubbles very happy.'

'So . . . if you'll sign right here,' he said to Mom, tapping his paper, 'I'll leave you a phone directory and be on my way.'

Mom signed and said, 'Thank you very much.'

'Don't mention it.' He looked over at Sally.'

'Goodbye, sister . . .'

'Goodbye,' Sally said, 'and don't forget your toothpick.'

'Sally!' Mom said.

'What?'

The telephone man shook his head and went out the door.

'Oh . . . never mind,' Mom said.

'Can I make the first call?' Sally asked. 'Pretty please . . .'

'Who are you going to call?'

'Barbara . . . I want to find out what's new in school.'

'She won't be home yet . . . it's just one-thirty.'

'Oh.'

'But you can call her later.'

'As long as I get to try it out before Douglas,' Sally said.

'Okay . . . you can be the first,' Mom said.

'Thanks!'

Sally looked up Barbara's number in the directory. She wrote it down and waited until three-fifteen, then she dialled. Barbara answered.

'Hi, it's me . . .' Sally said. 'I'm trying out our new phone . . . how does it sound to you? . . . oh, I had Virus X . . . but I'm better now . . . what's new in school? . . . really? . . . a new girl . . . what's she like? . . . oh . . . from Chicago . . . really a blood disease . . . oh . . . um, let's see . . . it's Central 4–6424 . . . okay . . . I'll be right here, waiting . . .'

Sally hung up the phone. 'She's going to call me back,' she told Mom.

'I have to do some shopping,' Mom said. 'I'll only be gone an hour. Do you need anything, Ma?'

'Corn flakes,' Ma Fanny said. 'And maybe another quart of milk . . .'

'Okay . . .' Mom said. 'Rest up, Sally.'

'I will.'

The phone rang. One long followed by two short rings. 'I'll get it,' Sally said, 'it's probably Barbara.' She lifted the receiver off the hook. 'Hello . . . oh, hi . . . I knew it would be you . . .'

'I've got information about Darlene,' Barbara said, 'but I had to wait for Marla to go outside so she wouldn't know I was telling you. Darlene's in ninth grade, she belongs to the Model Airplane Club, she's always on a diet, her father's a movie producer, they have a butler and two maids, they have three cars, one is a convertible, and she's not popular with the kids at school . . . listen, I've got to hang up now . . . see you tomorrow . . . bye . . .'

'Wait . . .' Sally started to say, but it was too late. She looked at Ma Fanny. 'I forgot to ask if I missed a lot of work in school . . .'

'So, you'll call her back,' Ma Fanny said. 'I'll be in the kitchen, making you another drink . . .'

Sally lifted the receiver again. But this time, instead

183

of the dial tone, she heard Bubbles talking. She hadn't realized she'd be able to hear the other people on their line. How interesting! Bubbles was talking to a boy. Sally held the receiver to her ear. Bubbles said, 'I don't know how I'll live until Saturday night.' The boy said, 'I think of you every second . . . I can't think of anything else.' Bubbles said, 'Can you get the car?' The boy said, 'I've got it all arranged.'

Ma Fanny came back into the living-room, carrying an orangeade for Sally. Sally replaced the receiver. 'I was trying to get Barbara,' she said, 'but the line was busy.'

Ma Fanny nodded.

That night, after supper, Mom placed a call to Daddy. Douglas and Sally each got to say hello. Then, when Mom took the phone, Douglas automatically went out the door. Mom told Sally, 'Go out to play now . . .'

'I can't,' Sally said. 'I have Virus X . . . remember?'

'Then go to the bathroom.'

'I don't have to.'

'Go anyway . . .'

'Oh . . .' Sally said, stomping across the living-room, through the sleeping alcove and into the bathroom.

She heard Mom sigh. 'She's such a funny little girl . . . always afraid of missing out . . . and I miss you too, Arnold . . . Sally, will you *close* the bathroom door, please!'

The next day Sally went back to school. She met Jackie, the new girl, during recess. Jackie was small

184

and frail, with very pale skin and long straight dark hair. 'My brother, Douglas, had nephritis,' Sally said.

'I'm sorry to hear that,' Jackie answered.

'He's okay now.'

'That's good.'

'So what did you have?'

'Mine's very complicated . . . it doesn't have a name . . . it's got to do with my blood . . .'

'Oh.'

'I was in the hospital three months . . . I almost died.'

'That sounds serious.'

'Yes . . . that's what everyone said . . . but I'm going to be all right now . . . my mother promised . . .'

While they were talking Peter ran up to Sally and pulled her braids. 'Oh . . . he makes me so mad!'

'I think he's cute,' Jackie said. 'I wouldn't mind if he pulled my hair.'

Andrea was sick for a week. One afternoon Sally asked Mom if she could go to the park with Shelby.

'Walking or riding?' Mom asked.

'Riding . . . but we'll be very careful.'

'And be back by five on the dot?'

'Yes, five on the dot . . . I promise,' Sally said.

Sally and Shelby rode to the park and watched Georgia Blue Eyes and his friends play ball.

Shelby said, 'I really want to kiss him . . . don't you?'

'I wouldn't mind,' Sally answered.

'We could chase him until he drops,' Shelby suggested, 'and then both of us could jump on him and you could hold him still while I kiss him and then I'd hold him still for you . . . what do you think?'

'I don't want to kiss him *that* much,' Sally said.

'Oh, well . . . too bad . . .'

They circled the field on their bicycles, then tried out a new bike path. 'Watch this . . .' Shelby said, pedalling faster and faster. 'No hands . . .'

'Be careful,' Sally called, trying to catch up with Shelby. But it was too late. Shelby fell and her bicycle toppled over her. 'Oh, no . . .' Sally jumped off her bicycle and freed Shelby. 'Are you okay?' she asked.

'No,' Shelby whimpered.

'What hurts?'

'Everything.' Shelby began to cry. 'Everything hurts . . .'

Shelby's knees and one elbow were badly scraped and bleeding. 'Oh, boy . . .' Sally said, 'are you going to have good scabs!'

That made Shelby cry harder.

'Can you ride?' Sally asked.

'No . . . how can I ride . . . I'm bleeding.'

'Well . . .' Sally thought fast. 'You stay right here and don't move an inch. I'll go for help and be right back.'

Shelby nodded and squeezed her nostrils together to keep them from dripping.

Sally hopped on her bicycle and took off. As she rounded the corner of the path she spotted Mr Zavodsky on a bench, reading his newspaper. Don't look up, Sally said under her breath. Don't notice me . . . just keep reading your paper. I don't have time for you now, Adolf . . . I've got other things to worry about, like Shelby . . . She rode with her head down and her shirt collar up. What good luck, she thought as she passed him, he didn't see me. She checked her new Mickey Mouse watch. It was two minutes to five. Mom would be really angry if she was late. She pedalled as fast as she could, all the way home. When she got there she burst in the door, calling, 'Mom . . . Mom!'

'What is it . . .' Mom asked, 'and do you know you're five minutes late?'

'Shelby fell off her bike and she's bleeding.'

'Where?'

'Her knees and her elbow . . .'

'I mean, where is she?' Mom said.

'In the park . . . I told her to stay right there and I'd get help.'

'You left her in the park . . . bleeding?'

'Well, you told me to be home by five . . .'

'But Sally . . . how could you leave your friend that way . . . I'm surprised at you . . . how would you feel if you'd had an accident and Shelby left you alone?'

'I didn't know what else to do,' Sally said.

'So now *I* have to go to the park . . . is that right?' Mom asked.

'Well, yes . . .' Sally didn't understand her mother. She'd come home for help. What else should she have done?

Mom ran into the bathroom, muttering, and threw some supplies into a paper bag. 'Okay . . . let's go.'

'To the park?' Sally asked.

'Honestly, Sally . . .' Mom let the screen door slam and raced down the stairs.

Sally followed.

'How are we going to get there?' she asked, trying to keep up with her mother.

'On bicycles,' Mom said.

'Both of us on mine?'

'No . . . I'll ride Douglas's.'

'You know how to ride a boy's bike?'

'Of course.'

'I never knew that.'

'There are many things you don't know.'

They rode to the park, side by side. Mom gathered her skirt between her legs and after a wobbly start became more sure of herself and rode as fast as Sally.

Sally led her mother to the bicycle path where she had left Shelby, but both Shelby and her bicycle were gone.

'Well . . .' Mom said. 'Where is she?'

'I don't know.' But Sally had an idea – an idea so horrible it was almost too scary to think about. *Mr Zavodsky.* He had found Shelby. Yes, he had found her lying there, helpless and bleeding. And then, when he saw that she was wearing a Jewish star around her neck he couldn't control himself anymore. He reached into his pocket and pulled out a rope. He tied it around Shelby's neck, pulling it tighter and tighter, until Shelby's face turned blue. She died with her eyes open, staring into space. And then, while her body was still warm, Mr Zavodsky pulled out his knife, sharp and shiny, and he peeled off Shelby's skin, slowly, so as not to rip any. And then he went home to make a new lampshade.

'Sally . . . what *is* wrong with you?' Mom asked.

'What . . . me . . . nothing . . .' Sally said.

'You look funny . . .'

'It's Shelby . . . I . . .'

'Now you see why you shouldn't have left her?'

'Oh, yes,' Sally said, unable to hold back her tears. 'And I'm sorry . . . I really am . . .'

'I know you are,' Mom said. 'You must never leave the scene of an accident. Do you understand that?'

'Yes . . .'

Mom put her arm around Sally. 'It's all right now . . . you've learned your lesson . . . stop crying and let's go . . .'

'It's not all right . . .'

'It will be . . . once we find Shelby.'

'But we can't . . . she'll be . . .'

'We can and we will . . . and when we do, we'll tell her we're sorry . . .'

'But you don't understand . . .'

'We'll go to her house first,' Mom said. 'Her grandmother is probably worried sick.'

'But Mom . . .' Who should Sally tell first . . . Shelby's mother or her father? And how would she ever find them? All she knew was they lived somewhere in New York. They'd be sorry now . . .

189

sorry they'd spent so much time fighting over Shelby . . .

'Follow me, Sally . . . and no more buts . . .'

Sally could just imagine what would happen next. Shelby's grandmother would answer the door and say, *Hello, Sally . . . come in . . . come in . . . have a cookie . . . have a piece of Challah, fresh from the oven . . .*

Then Sally would say, I *really can't stay, Mrs Bierman . . . you see, I've come with bad news . . . very, very bad . . .*

Mrs Bierman would clutch her chest and Sally would take a big breath and say, *I'm sorry to tell you that Shelby has been murdered by Adolf Hitler.* No need to tell Mrs Bierman the gruesome details.

Adolf Hitler? Mrs Bierman would say, unbelievingly.

Yes.

Not the *Adolf Hitler?*

The very same one.

But how?

He came here to retire, you see.

Oh, I didn't know.

Nobody does.

Then Mrs Bierman would begin to cry. She would sob and yell and scream and beat her fists against the wall.

It's all my fault, Sally would tell her. *I hope you'll forgive me some day but if you won't I'll understand because I know you're old and Shelby is all you had in the whole world and now there's nothing left to live for . . . but I really didn't do it on purpose . . . in fact, I was sure I was doing the right thing . . . going home to get my mother and all . . . but now I realize that I must never ever leave the scene of an accident . . . and maybe I should have gone straight to the police about Mr Zavodsky . . .*

Zavodsky . . . who's Zavodsky?

That's what Hitler calls himself now . . . but you see, the police would want evidence . . . they always do . . . and until Shelby's murder we didn't have any . . . now, of course, they'll arrest him and stick him in the electric chair where he belongs and he won't kill any more children, ever.

Mrs Bierman would nod.

Maybe you could adopt a poor orphan from Europe and then you'd have someone to live for again . . .

'Here we are,' Mom said. 'Which apartment?'

'2C,' Sally said, feeling her legs shake.

Mom rang the bell.

Shelby's grandmother answered. 'Hello, Sally,' she said. 'Come in . . . come in . . . have some Challah, fresh from the oven . . .'

Sally shook her head. 'I really can't stay . . .' she began, but then, as Mrs Bierman opened the apartment door all the way, Sally saw Shelby, sitting on the floor, shooting marbles. 'Hi,' she said. 'I got tired of waiting in the park so I rode home. Granny cleaned up my knees . . . there were pebbles stuck to them.'

'I had *some* job,' Mrs Bierman said.

Sally started to cry again.

'What's wrong with you?' Shelby asked.

'Nothing . . .'

'Listen,' Shelby said, 'I'm really sorry . . . Granny

191

told me it wasn't right that I left the park after you went to get help for me . . . she explained how I should have waited right there until you came back . . . and we've been calling your house . . . but your grandmother didn't know where you were . . .'

'That's not it,' Sally said, fighting to control herself.

'Then what?'

'I thought you were dead, that's what!'

'God forbid!' Mrs Bierman said.

'God forbid!' Mom repeated, and then, sounding embarrassed, she added, 'Sally has an active imagination.'

'Such an imagination!' Mrs Bierman shook her head.

Shelby laughed and laughed. 'Why would I be dead? I just fell off my bicycle . . . you don't die from that . . . that's the silliest thing I ever heard.' She shot her black marble across the room. It hit Sally in the foot.

Dear Mr Zavodsky,
I know what you were thinking of doing to Shelby
today. I always know what you are thinking! Any
day now I will have the evidence I need and then
you will get what you deserve!

Chapter 19

Before Miss Beverly dismissed the Saturday morning ballet class she announced a contest, sponsored by Raymond's Shoe Store. Raymond's had the very pair of pink satin toe slippers that Margaret O'Brien had worn while filming *The Unfinished Dance*. Sally had now seen the movie three times and it was still her favourite. Everyone who took ballet lessons in Miami Beach was invited to try them on. And the person who fit best into Margaret O'Brien's shoes would win the contest and get a free trip to Hollywood – *and* a screen test – *and* lunch with Margaret herself!

Sally just *had* to win. Then she would be discovered and get to be a famous movie star too. And when she caught Virus X again, it would say so in all the papers, including *The Forward*. And Miss Swetnick would say, *Isn't it wonderful . . . two girls from my class becoming famous in the same year . . . Barbara Ash for spelling and Sally Freedman for the movies!*

'Let's go over to Raymond's right after lunch,' Andrea said, as she and Sally walked home from ballet class. They each carried a package. Andrea hugged hers and said, 'Don't you just love our new ballet dresses?'

'They're okay,' Sally said, shifting her package from one arm to the other. She tried to hide her disappointment, because instead of the pink net tutu she'd been hoping for, her ballet dress turned out to be white cotton, with red smocking.

'In Brooklyn I had this ugly exercise outfit for acrobatics,' Andrea said. 'A blue skirt and a beige jersey top. This one is beautiful. We're so lucky!'

'In New Jersey I had a pink dotted Swiss ballet dress.'

'Dotted Swiss!' Andrea said. 'That's so fancy.'

'I went to a fancy dancing school.' Sally couldn't tell if Andrea was impressed or if she thought *fancy* meant bad. 'My teacher had ballet slippers in every colour.'

'Even red?'

'Yes . . . and green and blue and yellow, too.'

'I never saw ballet slippers in those colours . . .' Andrea said, giving Sally a sceptical look.

'Well, Miss Elsie had them . . . you can ask my mother . . . and a different ballet costume every week, to match her slippers . . .'

'Hmmm . . . I'll bet you anything my feet will fit into Margaret O'Brien's toe slippers,' Andrea said.

'What makes you so sure?'

'We have the same build . . . haven't you noticed?'

'No,' Sally said.

'Take a good look.' Andrea stood still.

Sally looked her up and down. 'I can't remember Margaret O'Brien's build.'

'I'm surprised you haven't noticed how much alike we look,' Andrea said.

'Who . . . you and me?'

194

Andrea made a sound with her tongue. 'No . . . me and Margaret O'Brien.'

Sally hid a smile.

'You don't think so?' Andrea asked.

'Nope.'

'We both have dark hair . . .'

'So does Hitler.'

Andrea spat. 'How many times have I told you *never* to say that name in front of me!' She spat again.

'I'm sorry . . . I forgot . . .'

'You better spit, Sally . . . you better spit right now or I'm never speaking to you again.'

'Okay . . . okay . . .' Sally went to the curb and worked up some saliva. Then she took a big breath. 'Hoc-tooey,' she said, spitting into the street. At the same moment, a bird, flying overhead, plopped on Sally's arm. 'Look at this!' she said to Andrea.

'Eeuuwww . . .' Andrea held her nose. 'How disgusting!'

'That's how much you know . . .'

Sally ran the rest of the way home. When she got there she raced up the stairs, kicked open the door, tossed her package on the floor and shouted, 'Look at this . . . a bird made on me . . . look . . .' She held out her arm for Douglas and Mom and Ma Fanny to see.

Ma Fanny clapped her hands together. 'Good luck for a year!' she said, hugging Sally. 'And it couldn't happen to a better person.'

'It's not just superstition . . . is it?' Sally asked.

'No more than *knock on wood* or *bad things always happen in threes*,' Douglas said, sarcastically.

'Good luck for a year,' Ma Fanny repeated. 'You can take it or leave it.'

'I'll take it!' Sally thought of what this could mean. That her father would be all right. That the police would arrest Mr Zavodsky. That she'd win the contest at the shoe store. That Miss Swetnick would start asking her easier words during spelling bees. That Georgia Blue Eyes would kiss her, voluntarily. That Peter Hornstein would grow up into a Latin Lover and want *her* for his partner. That Big Ted would give Daddy such good tips in the stock market they'd get rich. That Harriet Goodman would get transferred to another class. That . . .

'So . . . I'm going to the Roney,' Douglas said, stretching.

'Not so fast,' Mom told him. ' . . . I haven't decided yet.'

'When we were interrupted by Miss Bird Crap . . .'

'Douglas!'

'When my dear, sweet little sister came home we were in the midst of a . . .'

'We were *discussing* the situation,' Mom said.

'Some discussion!' Douglas said. 'It was more like the Spanish Inquisition . . .'

'What's that?' Sally asked.

'Mind your own business, for once!' Douglas told her.

'You know,' Mom said, 'I'm on your side, Douglas.'

196

'Good . . . then it's all settled . . .'

'Such a *swell* my son picks for his friend,' Mom said, sounding half-annoyed and half-pleased.

'I don't get you,' Douglas said to Mom. 'First, it's *Douglas, make friends . . . try harder . . . don't sit around by yourself so much* . . . so I find a friend . . . so now all I hear is *The Swells* . . . so they're rich . . . so what's wrong with that . . . aren't you the one who's always saying it's just as easy to fall in love with a rich person as a poor one?'

'That's enough, Douglas!' Mom said and Sally could tell by the look on her face that she wasn't just angry but that her feelings were hurt too.

'When you can't think of anything better to say it's always, *That's enough, Douglas!*' He mimicked Mom and sounded surprisingly like her.

'Dougie . . .' Ma Fanny said, 'don't talk like that to your mother . . . she loves you . . .'

'Love-schmov . . .' Douglas retreated to the bathroom.

'What am I going to do with that boy?' Mom asked.

'Sha . . .' Ma Fanny said, 'everything will turn out fine . . . he's a good boy . . . he's got growing pains, that's all.'

'Does it hurt when your bones begin to grow fast?' Sally asked.

'It hurts inside,' Ma Fanny said.

'How about breasts . . . does it hurt when they start to grow?'

'You shouldn't be thinking about breasts at your age,' Mom said.

'Why not? Some girls in my class have them already . . . and take a look at Andrea . . . she wears a bra . . . did you know that . . . and she's just one year older than me.'

'They don't hurt, mumeshana . . .' Ma Fanny said. 'They grow quietly, when they're ready.'

Mom cleared her throat. 'Sally . . . go and wash off your arm before it starts to smell.'

'But I can't . . . then I won't have good luck for a year.'

Ma Fanny laughed. 'All that counts is the bird picked *you* . . . nothing can stop your good luck now . . .'

'Oh . . . I didn't know that,' Sally said. She went to the kitchen to wash because Douglas was still locked in the bathroom and she didn't want to mess with him.

Sally and Andrea stood on line at Raymond's Shoe Store. There were just nine more girls ahead of them. They'd been waiting for thirty-five minutes. Sally could feel the sweat trickling down her back. She thought of Douglas, swimming at the Roney Plaza, and of Shelby, holding her nose and sitting on the bottom of the Seagull Pool, and of the ocean, with the tide rushing in.

'Boy, am I thirsty,' Andrea said.

'Same here.'

'I could really go for a tall glass of orange juice, couldn't you?'

'Make mine grape,' Sally said, licking her lips.

'Oh . . . I always forget about you and the pulp.'

Ten minutes later it was Andrea's turn to try on Margaret O'Brien's ballet shoes. She sat down and kicked off her sandals. Sally stood at her side. Would Andrea's foot fit? Would she win the contest? Sally hoped not. She knew it was wrong to wish Andrea bad luck but she wanted to win so much. If *she* couldn't win the contest then she certainly didn't want Andrea to win.

The shoe man held out the slipper. Andrea slid her foot in as far as it would go but the heel was still sticking out. 'Oops . . .' the shoe man said. 'It's a little too small for you . . . sorry, sweetheart . . . next,' he called.

'Right here,' Sally said.

'Listen,' Andrea said. 'It's not really too small for me. Miss Beverly told us toe shoes should hug the foot . . . and if I just bend my toes a little . . .'

'Really, sweetheart . . . take it from your Uncle Joe . . . it's just not your size . . .'

'You're not my uncle,' Andrea said, standing up and pouting.

She and Sally changed places. Sally knew exactly how Cinderella must have felt when it was her turn to try on the glass slipper. She closed her eyes for a minute. Thank you, bird . . . thank you for choosing me to plop on. She took off her sandal and held out her foot, digging her fingernails into the upholstered arms of the chair. The shoe man held out Margaret's pink slipper. It didn't have a boxed toe, like Sally's toe shoe. This toe was covered with satin, like a professional ballerina's. She eased her foot into the shoe. It fitted! She didn't have to bend her toes or anything. Her whole foot went in easily. She smiled. But, wait . . . there was too much space *around* her foot. Maybe the shoe man wouldn't notice. 'It's very comfortable,' Sally said, glancing at Andrea. Andrea looked concerned. Her lips were scrunched up and her brow was wrinkled. She doesn't want me to win, Sally thought. She doesn't want me to win any more than I wanted her to win.

'Sorry, sweetheart . . .' the shoe man said to Sally. 'It's too wide for your narrow little foot.'

'I could stuff the sides with lamb's wool,' Sally said, 'I usually do that anyway.'

'Lamb's wool is okay for the toe, sweetheart . . . but not for the rest of the foot . . . don't look so glum . . . maybe you'll win some other time . . . next,' he called and Sally knew it was over, that she had to put her sandal on and stand up and let someone else try on Margaret O'Brien's toe slipper.

She felt like crying. Some good luck that bird was bringing her! She couldn't speak. If she did her voice would break and then nothing would stop the tears. And she wasn't going to make a fool of herself like that blonde girl in the corner, bawling her eyes out.

She and Andrea went outside. 'Who wants a trip to Hollywood anyway?' Andrea asked. 'All they let you eat there is parsley sandwiches.'

'Says who?'

'I read it in a movie magazine . . . they feed all the movie stars parsley sandwiches so they'll stay skinny. Imagine no bologna or cupcakes or spaghetti . . .'

'I don't like spaghetti,' Sally said.

'But you like bologna, don't you?' Andrea said.

'Yes . . . and cupcakes too.'

'Well, then . . .'

'That bird didn't bring me good luck at all,' Sally told Ma Fanny. They were in the breakfast nook waiting for Douglas to return from the Chinese restaurant with a take-out supper.

'How do you know it's not good luck?' Ma Fanny asked.

'I didn't win the contest, did I?'

'But in the long run that could be good luck.'

'How?' Sally asked.

'Suppose you won,' Ma Fanny said. 'Suppose you went to Hollywood and while you were there the hotel burned down, God forbid . . .'

'I don't get it,' Sally said.

'Think, mumeshana . . . think and you'll understand.'

Sally thought about what Ma Fanny had said but it still didn't make any sense to her.

Douglas came home with the food. Ma Fanny fixed the tea while Mom opened the containers – first the rice, then the noodles, and finally the chow mein. But when Mom saw the chow mein she screamed and put the lid back on its container.

'What . . . what is it . . . what's the matter . . .' they all asked at once.

'A cockroach,' Mom said. 'A cockroach right on top . . . sitting on the chow mein.' The colour drained from her face.

'Let me see that . . .' Douglas said. He opened the container slowly. 'Hot damn! Look at that . . .' He held the container open for Sally and Ma Fanny to see.

'Close it up, Douglas,' Mom said. 'For God's sake . . . close it up before he gets out . . .'

'I'm taking it back,' Douglas said. 'I'm taking it back and telling them what I think of their restaurant . . .'

'No, don't . . .' Mom said. 'We'll have tuna instead.'

'That's not the point,' Douglas said, his face turning more and more red. 'We can't let them get away with this . . . just because I'm only fourteen they can't put a cockroach in my chow mein and get away with it!'

He stormed out of the door, carrying the container of chow mein.

Mom called after him but Ma Fanny said, 'Let him go, Louise . . . let him handle it himself.'

'Ma Fanny . . .' Sally said.

'What, lovey?'

'Does it mean something special if you find a cockroach in your chow mein?'

'Yes . . .'

'What?'

'It means the chow mein comes from a very dirty restaurant!'

✳

Chapter 20

February 19, 1948

Dear Doey,

I am waiting and waiting for my luck to begin. I hope it starts soon because I sure could use it.

I hope you are feeling just fine. I am almost fine, except for the fungus on the bottoms of my feet. At first Mom said it came because I didn't dry between my toes, but then she changed her mind and decided it came from walking barefoot on the rug in the living-room. She says we don't know who rented this place before us and what kinds of germs they may have left. Dr Spear said my fungus came from the air. I believe him. He gave me a salve to rub into my feet three times a day and I have to wear white cotton socks until it is gone. Nobody, but nobody, wears socks to school here. I feel like a jerk!

Did you hear about the rain? It came down in buckets, as Ma Fanny would say. The gutters were flooded in a few minutes and all the big kids walked home from school carrying their shoes. They had so much fun! I can't wait to be a big kid. Mom almost killed Douglas though. She yelled that he would catch pneumonia or worse from getting his feet so wet. She made him soak them in a hot tub for an hour. He was so mad he didn't talk to her for two days!

Did you hear about Douglas's friend? Her name is Darlene. Mom calls her family The Swells because they

*are very rich, maybe even millionaires, and they belong
to the Roney Plaza instead of the Seagull Pool, like
us. Don't tell Douglas that I said this, but Darlene is
fat. My friend Barbara and I saw her outside the high
school one day, talking to Douglas. They are building
a model airplane together. Darlene reads every issue
of* Popular Science *and* Popular Mechanics *and she
is giving Douglas a subscription to* Model Airplane
News *for his birthday.*

*I understand why you can't come down for my
birthday. It will be more fair if you come in-between
mine and Douglas's, like you said. I am disappointed
but I will try to have fun anyway. I'll miss you a lot
at my party. Mom is taking me, Andrea, Barbara and
Shelby to The Park Avenue Restaurant. I'm going
to eat twenty bowls of whipped cream, at least! See
you soon.*
Love and kisses and a big treatment,
Your favourite and only daughter,
Sally F.

Besides the fungus and the fact that Daddy wouldn't
be down for her birthday, something else was bothering Sally – Peter Hornstein liked Jackie, the new
girl in her class.

Peter began to write notes to Sally.

How come you don't wear halters like Jackie?
How come you don't wear your hair like Jackie?
*How come you don't have tiddly winks, like
Jackie?*

205

This last note was the worst. All the boys in school called breasts *tiddly winks* and when Sally wore her pinafore with the open sides, they teased her all day. She was never going to wear it again! But Jackie didn't have anything to show either. She was just as flat as Sally, maybe even flatter because she was so skinny.

Peter was driving her crazy with his *how come* notes. Finally, Sally wrote one back to him. *If you like Jackie so much how come you don't write notes to her?*

He answered, *How come you care?*

More and more Sally found herself daydreaming about kissing Peter instead of Georgia Blue Eyes.

Besides the fungus and Daddy not coming down for her birthday *and* Peter liking Jackie, Sally was disturbed that Mr Zavodsky was still walking around a free man. It was time to do something about that!

Dear Chief of Police,
You don't know me but I am a detective from New Jersey. I have uncovered a very interesting case down here. I have discovered that Adolf Hitler is alive and has come to Miami Beach to retire. He is pretending to be an old Jewish man. He uses the name Zavodsky and lives at 1330 Pennsylvania Avenue. He is in disguise so don't expect him to look just like his pictures. I know that you want evidence. Well, I'm working on it. Any day now I will be able to give you the exact details. In the meantime I just wanted you to know what's going on. Do not put any other detectives on this case. If you do you might ruin . . .

Andrea was knocking on the door, calling, 'Sally . . . Sally . . .'

'Hi,' Sally said, letting her in.

'What're you doing?' Andrea asked.

'Writing a letter.'

'To who?'

'Oh . . . somebody you don't know . . .'

'Want to play potsy?'

'Sure.' Sally put her letter in her keepsake box and she and Andrea went outside.

The following Friday morning Sally woke up with a stomach ache. 'I warned you yesterday that too much bologna would make you sick,' Mom said.

'I only ate six pieces.'

'That's five pieces too many.'

'I won't do it again.'

'Ma Fanny and I are supposed to go to a Hadassah meeting this afternoon,' Mom said.

'I'll be better by then.'

'Don't worry, tootsie,' Ma Fanny said. 'I'd rather stay home with you any day.'

'Oh no, Ma,' Mom told Ma Fanny. 'If anybody has to stay home with her, it's me. I know how much you've been looking forward to today's lecture. She wouldn't listen when I told her to stop eating that bologna . . . and she stuffed herself full of pickles . . . how many did you have, Sally . . . four, five . . .'

'Just three,' Sally said.

'But I'll bet they were big dills, weren't they?'

'Pretty big.'

'I certainly hope you've learned a lesson.'

'I have ... I have ...' Every time Mom said bologna or pickles Sally felt worse.

At noon Precious Redwine came to iron. When Precious heard that Mom was going to miss her meeting because of Sally's stomach ache she said, 'I've got eight kids at home, Mrs Freedman ... so you go on and get ready and I'll watch Sally for you ...'

'Well, that's very kind of you, Precious,' Mom said. 'You're sure you don't mind?'

'I don't mind.'

'I feel better anyway,' Sally said. 'They were just gas pains.'

Mom touched Sally's forehead three more times before she left with Ma Fanny, telling Precious, 'If there's an emergency I can be reached at Temple Beth-El, on the corner of Fourteenth Street.'

'She'll be just fine ... don't you worry,' Precious said.

As soon as Mom and Ma Fanny left, Sally lay back on her day bed and made up a story inside her head ...

Esther Williams Finds a Sister

Esther Williams is searching for a girl to play her younger sister in a new movie. She comes to Miami Beach but she can't find anyone suitable at the Roney Plaza, so she tries the Seagull Pool. When she spots Sally, floating on her back, she says, *That's her ...*

that's the girl I want to play my little sister! We'll teach her to swim just like me. I can tell she's got real talent by the way she floats on her back. We'll need a boy to play opposite her . . . someone with dark, flashing eyes.

Oh, I know just the boy, Sally tells Esther Williams, and she introduces her to Peter Hornstein, who happens to be visiting at the Seagull Pool that very day. Then Sally and Peter fly off to Hollywood with Esther Williams and they have to practise kissing three times a week.

Sally sighed. 'What is it, sugar?' Precious Redwine asked, licking her finger, then touching it to the iron.

'Nothing . . .' Sally said.

The phone rang. Three short rings. Sally already knew that one long ring was Mrs Purcell, who lived in their building, but it wasn't much fun to listen in on her conversations because they were always about her headaches and backaches and hot flashes. And she knew the Daniels' ring too. One long, one short, then another long. She'd listened to Bubbles and her boyfriend plenty of times. But this was the first time she'd heard three short rings. She picked up the receiver very quietly and covered the mouthpiece with one hand, while raising it to her ear with the other.

'Hey, Zavodsky . . . that's you?' It was a man's voice.

'That's me, Simon,' Mr Zavodsky answered.

Sally sucked in her breath. She didn't know *he* was on their party line too. What good luck! At last the bird plop was working.

'So how's by you?' the man named Simon asked.

'By me, it's okay,' Mr Zavodsky said.

'By me, too.'

'So . . . it's all set for tonight?'

'All set . . . just like I promised,' Simon said.

'Good . . . so, you'll come by about eight?' Mr Zavodsky asked.

'About eight sounds good. We'll walk over from your place.'

'You should please be careful walking,' Mr Zavodsky said.

'I'm not always careful?' Simon asked.

'I should know?' Mr Zavodsky asked him.

'Goodbye.'

'Goodbye, yourself.'

Sally waited until she'd heard the click, then she replaced the receiver. It has to be a code, she thought. Yes, a secret code! Otherwise it made no sense. And Simon was probably one of Hitler's old cronies, from the war. And probably what they were planning for tonight at eight was somebody's murder!

'Why do you listen to other people on the telephone?' Precious Redwine asked.

'I like to,' Sally told her.

'You shouldn't do that.'

'I know.'

'It's not nice.'

'I know.'

'Then why do you do it?'

'I told you . . . I like to . . . I like to know what's going on . . .'

Precious Redwine laughed then – a big, deep laugh that came right out of her belly. 'You're a nosy little girl . . . you know that?'

Sally nodded. 'Please don't tell on me.'

'I won't tell on you if you don't tell . . .'

'Tell what?' Sally asked.

'That I'm going to sit down and have a little rest.'

'It's a deal,' Sally said.

Precious lowered herself into the big chair in the living-room, kicked off her shoes, and put her feet up on the footstool. 'Oh my . . . that feels good . . . off my aching feet at last . . .'

'You better not walk barefoot in here,' Sally said. 'There might be a fungus in our rug.'

'I've got tough old feet,' Precious said, closing her eyes.

There were so many questions Sally wanted to ask Precious Redwine, starting with her beautiful name. And then she wanted to ask about drinking from the *Coloured* water fountain and about riding in the back of the bus and about her eight kids and about how she learned to be such a good ironer and about how she touched her wet finger to the iron without burning herself and about which half of her was Seminole Indian . . . but while Sally was working up the nerve to speak, Precious fell asleep, and when she woke up, half an hour later, Sally had lost her nerve again.

So Precious went back to her ironing and Sally went back to *Esther Williams Finds a Sister, Part Two*.

Chapter 21

'But I have to go out tonight,' Sally told her mother. 'Just for a little while.'

'No . . . you stayed home from school with a stomach ache so you can't possibly go outside until tomorrow.'

'But Mom . . . my stomach ache is all better. It was all better before you left for your Hadassah meeting.'

'The answer is still *no*, Sally.'

'But Mom . . . it's very warm out and I'll come in by eight . . . I promise . . . and you always let me stay out until nine on Fridays.'

'Stop begging,' Mom said. 'If I let you go out you'll only run around and get all sweated up and then you'll get thirsty and want to drink a quart of juice and then, bingo, another stomach ache.'

'I won't run. I'll sit very quietly by the goldfish pool.'

'This discussion is over,' Mom said. 'Tonight you're going to bed early and that's that.'

If Sally couldn't go out tonight then she wouldn't get to see Mr Zavodsky's friend, Simon. And this could be just the evidence she'd been waiting for! But there was no point in arguing with her mother. Mom wasn't going to change her mind. Sally wrote another note.

Dear Mr Zavodsky,
Okay. Enough is enough! I know all about you and
Simon. You better not try anything funny. I'm
closing in on you. This is your last chance to give
yourself up.

Sally was going to put this letter into Mr Zavodsky's mailbox the next morning, on her way to the
Seagull Pool Club. But the Rubins had recently
joined the Seagull and today was to be their first day
and both families were going over together. So there
was no chance for Sally to mail her letter without
being noticed. She would just have to wait until
later.

'I'm so excited!' Andrea said. 'Do you like my
new suit?'

'It's very nice,' Sally said, putting the letter into
her beach bag. Andrea's new bathing suit was two-
piece, with green stripes. The top was the same kind
of halter that Jackie wore to school. The same
kind that Peter Hornstein admired.

When the girls were in the changing room at the
Seagull Sally told Andrea, 'You have to wear a
bathing hat here.'

'I hate bathing hats!'

'Me too . . . they make my head itch . . . but you
can't go in without one . . . it's a rule.'

'I hate rules!'

'Me too . . . and that's not the only one either . . .
you have to wash your feet before they'll let you
in . . .'

213

'My feet!'

'Yes.'

'You're the one with the fungus,' Andrea said.

'I have to wash mine too . . . besides, my fungus is cleared up . . . you want to see . . .' She sat on the bench and held her bare feet up so that Andrea could see the bottoms.

'They're peeling!'

'I know,' Sally said. 'That's the fungus part coming off.'

'Euueewww . . .' Andrea made her 'disgusting' face.

Sally was worried. She had never told Andrea that Georgia Blue Eyes belonged to the Seagull Pool. The only thing to do now was pretend that she had never seen him there before. She'd act as surprised as Andrea. Of course, she'd have to explain this to Shelby but she was sure Shelby would go along with her. Or better yet, maybe Georgia Blue Eyes wouldn't show up today. Maybe he'd stay home with Virus X or something.

Sally, Andrea and Shelby were dunking in the shallow end of the pool when four boys surrounded them. One of them was Georgia Blue Eyes! But before Sally had a chance to say anything he sneaked up behind Andrea and untied her bathing suit top. 'Tiddly winks . . . tiddly winks . . .' he called and the other boys joined in, chanting, 'Tiddly winks . . . tiddly winks . . .'

Luckily for Andrea her halter top was tied in two places, around her back *and* around her neck.

Georgia Blue Eyes got only the string around her back. Andrea held her suit to her as the boys splashed, cutting the water with their hands so that it hit the girls in their faces. 'Stop it . . . stop it . . .' the girls cried.

'Hey . . . it's Sally Nevermind,' Georgia Blue Eyes shouted. And the other boys began to call, 'Sal-ly Nevermin-d . . . Sal-ly Nevermin-d . . .'

Finally, the lifeguard blew his whistle and the boys swam away. They were still laughing when they reached the other side of the pool.

Andrea ran for the changing room, with Sally and Shelby on her trail. When they got there, safe at last, Sally could see that Andrea was close to tears. 'Want me to tie your top for you?' Sally asked.

'Don't you touch me!' Andrea said. '*He* knows your name.'

Sally was surprised that Andrea was angry about that now. What the boys did was so much worse. She was sure Andrea would be too mad at them to care about Georgia Blue Eyes knowing her name. 'No, he doesn't,' she told Andrea.

'Don't lie to me . . . I heard him call you *Sally*.'

'Oh, that . . . he knows my first name but not my last.'

'You never told me *he* belongs here!'

'I didn't know myself.'

'Liar!'

'I've seen him here a few times but I didn't know he was a member.'

'You never said you *saw* him here.'

215

'I didn't? I guess I forgot.'

'How could you . . . how could you keep such a secret from me? I hate you! I'm never going to speak to you again!' She ran into a toilet stall and slammed the door.

'Whew . . .' Shelby said, 'she's really mad.'

'I know.'

'I think she might *really* hate you.'

'I know.'

'Have you got any suntan lotion?' Shelby asked. 'My back is killing me.'

Sally opened her locker and took out her beach bag.

'What are you going to do?' Shelby asked.

'I don't know.' Sally couldn't find the lotion. She turned the bag upside down and shook. Everything fell out on to the wet floor, including her letter to Mr Zavodsky.

'I sure wouldn't want to trade places with you!' Shelby said.

Sally picked up her letter. It was ruined. The ink had blurred.

'Could you do my back?' Shelby asked.

'In a second . . .' Sally mashed up her letter and threw it into the trash basket. She could write a better one later. Right now she had other things to worry about, like Andrea hating her.

Sally got a letter from her father, written on pink dental wax, the same day that Douglas got one

216

written on toilet paper. Daddy never ran out of ideas for funny letters. Sally also got a letter from Christine.

Dear Sally,
You probably don't remember me but I used to be
your best friend. My name is Chrissy. We used to
live on the same street. I haven't heard from you in
ages. It is too bad that some people go away and
forget their old friends. In case you are wondering,
we survived the ice storm. My mother says it will
go down in history. In case you are wondering, we
have a new girl in our class. Her name is Pearl
and she comes from Ohio. She thinks she's great
because she can do fractions. Nobody likes her. She's
a real jerk. Do you remember Tommy Byers? In
case you're wondering, I like him. So does Pearl.
I guess you must be having a great time with all
the other millionaires. If you can find time to write,
in between all your parties and dances, I might be
able to find the time to read your letter.
Your old friend,
Chrissy

Miss Swetnick and Peter Hornstein's brother, Hank, rented an apartment in the building next to Sally's. Sally could look out her living-room window and see into their bedroom. They were painting it themselves. On Thursday after supper Sally waved to them and they waved back. 'Need any help?' Sally called. 'I love to paint.'

'Sure . . . come on over,' Hank called back, leaning

out the window. 'We're going to do the bathroom tonight.'

Sally ran next door. 'We have a *beautiful* bathroom back home,' she told Miss Swetnick and Hank. 'It's black and lavender.'

'We're doing ours in blue,' Miss Swetnick said. She had on shorts and a man's shirt, with the tails hanging out. Sally was used to seeing her in dresses.

'Black and lavender looks really pretty . . .' Sally said, 'just like a bordello.'

Miss Swetnick and Hank looked at each other and laughed. 'Who told you that?' Miss Swetnick asked.

'My father,' Sally said. 'Have you ever been to a bordello?'

'No,' Miss Swetnick said, 'I haven't.'

'Me neither.'

They laughed again. 'Do you know what a bordello is?' Hank asked.

'No . . . do you?'

Miss Swetnick cleared her throat and said, 'Come on . . . let's get busy . . . we have a lot to do tonight . . .'

They went into the bathroom. Hank handed Sally a paint brush. 'You can start under the sink,' he said. 'I can't get in there because of my size.'

'I'm going to work on the curtains, darling,' Miss Swetnick said.

'Okay . . .' Hank told her. 'My partner and I will see how far we can get . . .'

Sally crawled under the sink. 'Does your brother ever help you paint?'

'No . . . Peter would rather play ball.'

Sally dipped her brush into the tray of blue paint and started on the wall. 'Does Peter talk much about his school friends?'

'Not too much.'

Some paint dripped on to the floor. Sally wiped it up with a cloth. 'Does he ever mention them by name?'

'Now and then.'

Sally paused, her brush on the wall. 'Does he ever mention Jackie?'

'Jackie . . . let's see . . . is he the one who plays third base?'

'No . . . Jackie's a girl!'

'Oh, a girl! No, I don't think he's ever mentioned her . . .'

Sally smiled to herself and went back to painting.

After a while, Hank said, 'The only girl I've heard him talk about is Sally . . .'

'*Sally* . . . that's me!'

'Oh . . .' Hank said. 'I didn't realize you were *that* Sally.'

'Yes, I'm the only one in the class.' She wanted to ask, *What did Peter say about me?* but she just couldn't. That would be too nosy.

Miss Swetnick came back into the bathroom. 'I've got the curtains up . . . come and see . . .'

Sally and Hank followed Miss Swetnick into the bedroom. The new curtains were drawn, making the room dark.

219

'Very nice!' Hank said, putting his arms around Miss Swetnick's waist.

'They're pretty,' Sally said. 'I like the colours.' They were made out of heavy cotton material, in yellow, orange and brown print. 'But you won't be able to see into our living-room anymore.'

'Yes, we will . . .' Miss Swetnick said. 'See . . .' and she pulled the cord, opening the curtains.

'I meant you won't be able to see when the curtains are closed,' Sally said.

'Oh . . .' Miss Swetnick answered. 'I guess you're right.'

At eight o'clock, Sally said goodbye to Hank and Miss Swetnick. Too bad Hank hadn't told her anything else about Peter. Maybe next time.

'Thanks for helping,' Hank said.

'It was fun,' Sally answered. She was glad she'd done the hardest part for him. Getting the wall under the sink just right wasn't easy.

She had to walk to dancing class by herself, because Andrea still wasn't speaking to her. Sally had tried to explain. She'd said, 'I meant to tell you about him . . . I really did . . . it's just that I had so many other things on my mind . . . I forgot . . . that's all . . .'

'Don't waste your breath,' Andrea had said, 'because I'm not listening.'

Their mothers tried to get them back together but Andrea recognized this and told her mother to mind her own business. So their grandmothers tried to fix things up but Andrea saw through that too and told her grandmother to worry about her own friends.

On the way home from dancing school Sally tried again. 'Can I walk with you?' she asked Andrea.

Andrea didn't answer.

'Miss Swetnick is moving in next door.'

No response from Andrea.

'I'll tell you a secret . . .' Sally said, looking for some kind of expression on Andrea's face, but Andrea acted as if she hadn't heard a word. 'I like Peter Hornstein . . . nobody else in the whole world knows that, except maybe Barbara.'

Andrea didn't even look her way.

'I'd like to kiss him . . . I really would . . . Andrea, can you hear me?'

'No.'

'Remember the day we were walking home and the bird plopped on me?' Sally laughed, hoping Andrea would too. 'Andrea, please say something!'

'Something.'

They saw Omar at almost the same moment. He was lying in the middle of the street, in front of their building. Andrea cried out and ran to him. 'Omar . . . Omar . . .' She sank to her knees and gathered Omar's broken body into her arms. She held him close. 'Oh no . . . my baby . . . my poor baby . . .' She stroked his head. Omar's eyes were staring into space and his beautiful white fur was all bloodied. Sally knew he was dead.

Andrea sobbed, her body shaking, her cries growing louder and louder. Sally didn't know what to do, what to say. She touched Andrea's shoulder but Andrea shook her away. Sally ran into the house, calling, 'Omar's dead . . . Omar's dead . . .'

Andrea's mother heard Sally and so did many of the other neighbours. They all rushed outside, in time to see Andrea stand up and walk slowly toward the house, with Omar cradled in her arms.

'I didn't do it,' Mrs Richter said to no one in particular. 'I never liked that cat but I didn't do it.'

'Of course you didn't,' another woman said. 'You don't even have a car.'

'Hit and run . . .'

'Such a shame . . .'

'The poor child . . .'

'Getting his blood all over her dress . . .'

Mrs Rubin put her arms around Andrea and cried with her. Andrea's sister, Linda, became so hysterical her grandmother had to slap her and carry her upstairs.

'I'm sorry, Andrea,' Sally said, as Andrea walked by. 'I know how much you loved him.'

'No one will ever know how much I loved him,' Andrea wept.

Chapter 22

The phone rang. One long ring followed by two short rings. It was for them. Douglas answered. He'd been expecting Darlene to call. But it wasn't Darlene this time, because Douglas said, 'Yes . . . yes, this is the Freedman residence . . . just a minute, please . . .' He put the receiver down and called, 'Mom . . . hey, Mom . . . hurry up . . . it's long distance for you . . . person to person . . .'

Mom ran out of the bathroom, pulling her robe around her. 'Oh, my God . . . oh, my God . . . something's happened to Arnold . . .'

Ma Fanny rushed to her side and Sally and Douglas stood close by, waiting. Sally felt her stomach turn over. This is it, she thought. This is it. It's Daddy. Something terrible has happened. She wanted to scream. Scream because she'd been praying so hard. And for what? Barbara was right. It didn't help to pray. In that moment she knew she would never see her father again. Never feel his arms around her. Never give him another treatment. She let out a small cry, then clapped her hand over her mouth. *Bad* things always happen in threes, she thought. First, Omar . . . and now, Daddy . . .

'Yes, this is Louise Freedman,' her mother said into the telephone. Then, 'Bette . . . Bette, is that you?' She covered the mouthpiece with her hand and told the three of them, 'It's Bette.' They nodded. 'Yes,'

Mom continued, 'yes, I can hear you . . . yes, yes . . . what is it?'

Sally tried to swallow but found she couldn't.

'Oh, thank God,' Mom said. 'Thank God everything's all right.' She covered the mouthpiece again and told the family, 'It's all right.'

Sally tasted the beans she'd had for supper.

'Yes, I'm okay now,' Mom said, sounding stronger. 'I was just so worried getting a person to person phone call . . . oh, it's good to hear your voice, Bette . . . I miss you, too . . . how are you? . . . you do? . . . you are?' Mom turned to Ma Fanny. 'It's an addition,' she said. Ma Fanny slapped her hand against the side of her face. 'Oh, God . . . that's wonderful,' Mom said into the phone. 'I'm so happy for you . . .' She started to cry and handed the phone to Ma Fanny.

'Bette . . .' Ma Fanny said. 'So tell me the good news . . . I want to hear it straight from the horse's mouth . . . I couldn't be happier . . . for all the money in the world I couldn't be happier . . . When? . . . August? . . . I'll be there with bells on . . . mazeltov, my darling . . .' She handed the phone back to Mom.

'Jack . . .' Mom said, 'Jack, is that you? Congratulations! It's wonderful news . . . the best.'

An addition, Sally thought. What does that mean? It's got to be something good, they're all so happy. An addition. Maybe Aunt Bette has passed some kind of arithmetic test. No, that's silly . . . it has to be something else. I'm so sick of secrets! Why doesn't anybody ever tell me what's going on!

When Mom and Ma Fanny were off the phone, Douglas said, 'That's great news for them but, personally, I wouldn't want one.'

'I should hope not, at your age,' Mom said and she and Douglas and Ma Fanny laughed together.

So, Sally thought, Douglas understood about the addition too. So, she was the only one who didn't know. Well, she wasn't about to admit it. Then Douglas would make fun of her, saying her mind was a blank, or that she was just a baby. 'What will the addition look like?' Sally asked, figuring she could find out what it was by playing twenty questions.

'Who can say?' Ma Fanny answered. 'As long as it's healthy we won't complain.'

'I still can't believe it,' Mom said. 'Just when I was expecting the worst it turned out to be the best.'

'And she's already four months?' Ma Fanny asked.

'Yes, I guess she didn't want to get our hopes up until she was sure . . . remember last time?'

'How could I forget?'

'The last time, what?' Sally asked.

'The last time Aunt Bette was pregnant she lost the baby after two months,' Mom said.

'Oh . . . she's going to have a baby.' Suddenly it all made sense.

'You dummy!' Douglas said. 'What'd you think she was going to have, an elephant?'

'No!' Sally said. 'An addition!'

'It *is* an addition,' Mom said, 'an addition to the family.'

'Oh . . . an addition to the family,' Sally said. 'Now I get it.'

Mom gave Sally a hug. 'You're so funny sometimes . . .'

Later, while Mom was setting her hair, Sally asked, 'How does a woman get pregnant, anyway?'

'Oh, you know . . .' Mom said.

'But I don't . . .'

'Well,' Mom began, 'the husband plants the seed inside the wife . . .'

'I know about *that*,' Sally said. 'But how does he get the seed and where does he plant it?'

'Well . . .' Mom said. She made three more pin curls before she spoke again. 'I think you need a book to explain that part. Tomorrow I'll go to the bookstore and see what they have on the subject.'

'Tomorrow's Sunday.'

'Oh . . . you're right. Well, I'll go first thing Monday morning.'

'But Mom . . . I want to know now!'

'I can see that, Sally. But you'll just have to wait until Monday.'

'You mean you don't know either?'

'I know,' Mom said, 'it's just that I don't know how to explain it to you . . . if Daddy were here he would, but I'm not very good at those things . . .'

Dear Aunt Bette,
Congratulations! I'm very glad to hear that Uncle
Jack got the seed planted at last. It will be nice to
have a baby cousin. I hope it's a girl and that you
name her Precious, which is what I would like
my name to be. Monday, Mom is getting me a book
explaining how you got the baby made. I'm really
curious!
Love and other indoor sports,
Sally J. Freedman, your friend and relative.

Monday morning, on her way to school, Sally called, 'And Mom . . . don't forget about that book!'

That afternoon, Sally found a brown bag on her day bed. Inside was the book and a note from Mom saying, *Don't show this to Douglas!*

Chapter 23

Andrea refused to leave her room. Mrs Rubin was worried about her. She came to Sally's house to discuss the situation with Mom.

'Promise her a movie . . .' Mom suggested.

'I've already tried that.'

'A new dress?'

'That, too . . .'

'A record album?'

'Even that . . .'

'Hmmm . . . what about a sundae at Herschel's every night for a week?'

'I know what she needs,' Sally said, and Mom and Mrs Rubin looked up, as if remembering for the first time that she was sitting at the table too.

'What's that?' Mrs Rubin asked.

'Something to love . . . like a kitten.'

'What a nice idea,' Mrs Rubin said. 'I wonder if it would work?'

'It will . . . I just know it,' Sally said. 'And I'd like to be the one to give her the kitten.'

'I must say, Sally . . . that's very generous of you, considering the way Andrea's been treating you this week.'

'She had a right to be mad at me.'

'Maybe so . . . but she's carried it too far,' Mrs Rubin said.

'In a way I don't blame her, though,' Sally said.

★

Sally and her mother went to the pet shop next to the movie theatre, where *The Outlaw,* starring Jane Russell, was playing. 'Can we go to see it?' Sally asked.

'No.'

'Not today . . . maybe Friday night or Saturday, I mean . . .'

'Absolutely not,' Mom said.

'But why . . . it looks good . . .'

'Never mind why.'

'Because you can see down Jane Russell's blouse when she bends over?' Sally asked.

'Who told you that?'

'Douglas . . . he's going to see it.'

'Over my dead body!'

'Oh, please, Mom . . . don't tell him I said anything about it . . . he'll kill me.' Why did she have to go and open her big mouth? She'd promised Douglas she could keep his secret.

'I won't tell him how I found out,' Mom said.

'Anyway, I don't see what's so bad about looking down Jane Russell's blouse . . . when Vicki bends over you can do the same thing.'

'Sally!'

'Well, it's true. That night I sat next to her at The Park Avenue Restaurant I could look down her dress and see everything.'

'Sally!'

'What?'

'Stop talking that way.'

'What way?'

'You know very well what way!'

Sally chose a ginger kitten for Andrea and Mom didn't say one word about it having worms. Ma Fanny lined a basket with blue velvet and tied a matching blue ribbon on the handle. Sally put the kitten in the basket and went across the hall, to Andrea's.

Mrs Rubin said, 'She's still in her room.'

Sally walked through the living-room, past the kitchen, to Andrea's room. It was no bigger than the foyer closet in Sally's house in New Jersey but at least it was all Andrea's. Andrea was lying face down on her bed.

'Hi . . . it's me . . . Sally.' She put the basket on the floor. 'I'm sorry about Georgia Blue Eyes . . . I should have told you before . . . and I'm sorry about Omar . . . I didn't love him as much as you but I did love him.'

'I know you did,' Andrea said, into her pillow.

'Will you be my friend again?' Sally asked.

'Yes.'

'Good . . . I've got something to show you.'

'What?'

'You can't see it that way.'

Andrea rolled over and sat up. Sally was surprised at the way she looked, with dark circles under her eyes and her hair matted to the side of her face. Sally picked up the basket and put it on the bed, next to Andrea.

Andrea looked into the basket. 'Oh no . . .' She shook her head and began to cry.

'But . . .'

'Did they think I'd forget about him just like that?' She buried her face in her hands.

'No,' Sally said, 'and anyway, it was *my* idea, not *theirs*.'

'Take it away,' Andrea cried. 'Take it far, far away . . .'

'You're impossible, Andrea Rubin . . . you know that? You're really impossible! It's hard to even like you sometimes . . .' Sally picked up the basket and stomped out of Andrea's room. She was shaking all over. She went home.

Mom said, 'What a shame . . . I guess we'll have to take the kitten back.'

'Please, Mom . . . can't we keep him?' Sally asked.

At first Mom didn't answer and Sally took her silence to mean *maybe*. 'Just feel how soft he is,' Sally said.

Mom stroked the kitten. 'He is soft, isn't he?'

'Yes . . . and I'd take care of him . . . really . . . you wouldn't have to do a thing . . .'

'I know, honey . . . but we can't take a chance on a kitten . . . we have too many allergies . . .'

'Name one person in this family who's allergic to cats . . .'

'It could be dangerous for Douglas.'

'Baloney!' Sally said, holding back tears.

'I'm sorry,' Mom said. 'I really am.'

'If you meant that you'd let me keep him.'

'We shouldn't have bought him in the first place . . . not without asking Andrea . . .'

'But I wanted to surprise her.'

'Sometimes surprises don't work,' Mom said.

They sat down to a dairy supper. 'What's this about going to see *The Outlaw?*' Mom asked Douglas.

Sally put her spoon down. 'Don't look at me,' she said to Douglas, before he'd even glanced her way.

'I want you to stay away from that movie,' Mom told him.

'It's a cowboy story,' Douglas said. 'What's wrong with cowboys all of a sudden?'

'Nothing.'

'Then why can't I go?'

'We both know the answer to that, Douglas!'

'It's not like I've never seen a breast . . . you know.'

'Douglas!'

'Suppose I want to be a doctor . . . I'm going to have to see plenty of them then.'

'This has nothing to do with being a doctor,' Mom said.

'You act like there's something wrong with the human body.'

'There's a time and a place for everything.'

'I think I'll ask Dad about it when he calls on Sunday . . . I'll bet he'll let me go!'

'Children . . .' Ma Fanny said, holding up a bowl, 'have some more carrots . . . they'll make you see in the dark.'

★

'I can't trust you with anything,' Douglas said to Sally, after supper. They were on the floor, playing with the kitten.

'I didn't tell on you . . . it just came out . . .'

'You better learn how to keep secrets or you're going to wind up with no friends.'

'I have friends. I have Shelby and Barbara and Andr . . .'

'Guess again.'

Sally let the kitten nibble on her finger. 'I'm sorry . . . from now on I'm going to try harder. I'm going to learn how to keep secrets if it kills me . . . really.'

'This time it doesn't even matter,' Douglas said, 'because I'm going whether *she* likes it or not.'

Sally nodded.

The doorbell rang while Sally was getting ready for bed. She was in the bathroom, brushing her teeth, when Mom came to get her. 'It's Andrea,' Mom said.

Sally wiped her mouth with the corner of a towel and went into the living-room.

Andrea said, 'I hear you have to take the kitten back.'

'Yes.'

'Can I have another look?'

'Help yourself.'

The kitten was curled up in the basket, sound asleep. Andrea lifted him out and put her face next to his soft body. 'Hello, you little darling . . . hello, you precious angel . . .' She looked up at Sally. 'I think I'm going to call her Margaret O'Brien the Second, if that's all right with you.'

'But Andrea,' Sally said, suddenly laughing, 'it's a *boy* cat.'

'Oh . . . in that case I'll call *him* Margaret O'Brien the Second!' And she laughed with Sally.

Aunt Bette wasn't the only one pregnant. Two weeks later Andrea said, 'Did you hear about Bubbles?'

'No . . . what?'

'She's going to have a baby!'

'But how can she . . . she's not even married.'

'You don't have to be married,' Andrea said.

'But my book says . . .'

'Never mind what your book says . . . I'm telling you . . . you don't have to be married . . . and Bubbles did it with a *goy* . . . so now Mr and Mrs Daniels are sitting shivah . . . pretending Bubbles is dead . . . and I think it's horrible . . . she's their only child . . . God should punish them for what they're doing.'

'If she'd done it with a Jewish boy would they be sitting shivah?'

'No, silly . . . then they'd be making a wedding.'

'I don't get it,' Sally said.

'It's all very complicated.'

Sally went home and told her mother, 'My book was wrong. You don't have to be married to get a baby.'

'If you're a nice girl you do.'

'Isn't Bubbles a nice girl?'

'I don't want to talk about that.'

But everybody else in their house was talking about it. Sally listened to Mrs Purcell on their party line. She said, 'I'd do the same thing if, God forbid, one of my children ran off with a goy. Thank God I don't have to worry . . . all three are married very well.'

Ma Fanny and Andrea's grandmother were talking about it. 'And her with scarlet fever yet,' Andrea's grandmother said.

'A pox on them!' Ma Fanny said, pointing to the Daniels' apartment. 'Sitting shivah for Bubbles . . . meshuggeners!'

Sally had never seen her so angry.

'Fanny . . . don't be so hard on them,' Andrea's grandmother said. 'Remember, they're orthodox Jews . . . they're doing what they feel is right.'

'Orthodox, schmorthodox.'

'Listen,' Andrea's grandmother said, 'plenty of goys disown their children for marrying Jews . . .'

'Your child is your child,' Ma Fanny said, 'no matter what . . . I could tell you plenty, but I won't . . .'

Sally wished she would.

'So, you'll make a donation through the temple?' Andrea's grandmother asked.

'Not a penny . . . not one cent . . . they should only rot in there,' Ma Fanny said, her face tightening.

Mom and Mrs Rubin and Andrea's grandmother were going to pay a condolence call on the Daniels

235

that evening. Ma Fanny refused to join them, even though Mom said, 'They're our neighbours . . . how will it look?'

'They should only know what it's like to *really* lose a child! Whatever they think, I couldn't care less . . .'

'What did you mean?' Sally asked Ma Fanny, after the others had left. Sally was sitting in the big chair, a hank of wool wrapped around her outstretched arms.

Ma Fanny sat on the footstool, facing her, rolling a wool ball. 'About what, sweetie pie?'

Sally watched as the wool flew off her arms. 'About losing a child . . . you sounded like you knew about that.'

Ma Fanny nodded.

'You lost a child?'

She nodded again.

'I never knew that,' Sally said.

'It's not something I advertise.'

'When did it happen?'

'A long time ago . . . before your mother was born . . . I had a baby boy and one day he died . . .' She snapped her fingers. 'Just like that!'

'From what?'

'We never found out . . . he was only five months old . . . his name was Samuel . . .' She sighed. 'Such a long time ago . . .'

'Is it a secret?' Sally asked.

'Not a secret . . . just something I don't like to talk about.'

'Thank you for telling me, Ma Fanny. I understand better now.'

Ma Fanny cupped Sally's chin in her hand. 'You're worth a million . . . you know that . . . more even . . .' She went back to winding her wool.

Chapter 24

Class 5B was having an election for King and Queen of Posture. The winners would go on to compete in the All-Fifth-Grade contest and the winners of that election would represent the entire fifth grade in the All-School contest. Barbara had nominated Sally, and Peter had seconded the motion, so Sally stood out in the corridor with the other five nominees, waiting, while the rest of the class voted.

In a few minutes Miss Swetnick opened the door and said, 'You can come back in now . . .'

The winners' names were written on the blackboard. *Gordon and Beatrice, King and Queen of Posture of Class 5B.* Sally tried to hide her disappointment. On her way back to her desk Harriet Goodman leaned over and said, 'I didn't vote for you . . . I'd *never* vote for you!'

'I'd never vote for you, either,' Sally answered.

She took her seat. Barbara whispered, 'You got six votes . . . that's pretty good . . . you came in third . . .'

Third and last, Sally thought. But at least she hadn't lost by just one vote. Then she'd have even more reason to hate Harriet. And, there was always next time. Maybe she'd do better then. There were so many contests in Miami Beach. The newspapers were full of them. *Miss Bright Eyes, Miss Complexion, Miss Long Legs.* Even Central Beach Elementary School had contests all the time. *Girl of the Week,*

Tumbler of the Month, Smile of the Year. Maybe they'd have a *Queen of Toenails* contest, Sally thought. Yes, she could win that one. Then she'd get to be fifth-grade representative to the *All-School-Queen of Toenails* election. And if Harriet Goodman didn't vote for her this time it wouldn't matter because everybody else in the class would. She looked down at her feet and wiggled her toes. She *did* have nice toenails!

'Sally . . .' Miss Swetnick said, 'would you please take out your arithmetic book and open to page ninety-two.'

When Sally got home from school she found Mr Zavodsky sitting on the porch with another old man. This one had white hair, suntanned skin and wore a flowered cabana shirt. Simon! Yes, it had to be. They were sharing some kind of book – reading, pointing and laughing together. Mr Zavodsky was so involved he didn't offer her candy, didn't even notice her.

'Look . . .' Mr Zavodsky said to Simon, tapping a page of his book. 'Do you remember her?'

'Do I remember her?' Simon answered. 'She's one I'll never forget!'

Their scrapbook of the war! Sally thought, running into the lobby and up the stairs. She tore a piece of paper from her notebook and scribbled:

Dear Mr Zavodsky,
I have seen you with Simon. His cabana shirt and
suntan may fool some people but not me. He is
the monster who was in charge of Dachau! I know

plenty about Dachau and what you and Simon did
to the prisoners there. You will pay for laughing
about it.

I'll copy this note over later, she thought. For now she folded it in half and put it in her keepsake box. She'd have to hurry. Andrea would be waiting to play potsy.

Daddy made some money on one of Big Ted's stock tips and came down to visit for five days in March, and again, over Easter vacation.

Sally was curled up in his lap, running her middle finger up and down his arm. She felt happy and relaxed like Andrea's kitten when he purred. ' . . . and the recreation room is almost finished,' Daddy said. 'All that's left to do is the floor and the trimmings . . . what do you think of green and black tiles?'

'Alice Ingram has red and black.' She wondered how long it would take to count all the hairs on his arm.

'Everybody has red and black . . . that's why I thought of green and black . . . but if you don't like green . . .'

'Oh no . . . green is nice . . .'

'And green leather on the built-in seats . . .'

'I like green a lot.'

'And a green top on the bar . . .'

'We can call it the Green Room,' Sally said. Daddy smiled at her.

240

'Can I have a party in it right away . . . as soon as I get home?'

'I think you should wait an hour or two.'

'You know what I mean,' Sally said, laughing.

'As soon as you want.'

'And can I have boys, too?'

'We better discuss that with your mother.'

'Why . . . what's wrong with having boys?'

'Nothing . . .'

'Then why do we have to ask Mom?'

'Okay,' Daddy said. 'You can have boys to your party.'

'Thanks . . . but the boy I like is here, in Miami Beach.'

'Then you don't have to have boys to your party after all.'

'But I might find some boys to like when I get back to New Jersey.'

'Then you *can* invite boys to your party . . .'

'Oh, Doey . . . you're being so silly!'

'Who's being silly?' he asked, tickling her in the ribs.

Ma Fanny called, 'Supper . . .'

Daddy sniffed in three times. 'Could that wonderful, fragrant aroma emerging from the depths of the kitchen by any chance be Fantastic Fanny's Fabulous Borscht?' he asked, leaping to his feet so that Sally rolled off his lap on to the floor. He scooped her up and flung her over his shoulder.

'Put me down . . . put me down . . .' Sally cried, loving every minute of her father's nonsense.

241

As they sat down to eat, Ma Fanny said, 'I don't know one single person who enjoys his borscht as much as you, Arnold . . .' She reached over and pinched his cheek as if he were a little boy.

Sally wished she could learn to like borscht. It looked so pretty – bright pink soup with tiny white potatoes floating in it. But the taste – cold beets – ugh! She drank a glass of tomato juice instead.

While the rest of them were enjoying their borscht, Mom said, 'Didn't you leave your recipe with Bette, Ma . . . so she could make it for Arnold?'

'More or less,' Ma Fanny said. 'I told her, a pinch of this . . . a pinch of that . . .'

'Bette tries hard,' Daddy said, 'but her pinches aren't like your pinches yet . . .' Now *he* leaned over and gave one back to Ma Fanny. 'Only you make the real thing . . . the genuine article . . .'

'How did I get myself such a son-in-law?' Ma Fanny asked.

'You were lucky,' Sally said.

'Sometimes I think he married me for my mother,' Mom said, and it didn't sound like she was joking.

At the end of the meal, when Daddy was sipping his coffee, he said, 'I have an announcement to make.'

'Yes . . .'

'What is it?'

'Tell us . . .'

'No,' Daddy said, 'I think I'll make you guess . . .'

'Oh, Doey . . .'

'You first, Sally.'

'What am I supposed to guess?'

'Guess where we're going . . .'

'Umm . . . Monkey Jungle?'

'Nope . . . your turn, Douglas.'

'To see *The Outlaw*?'

'Douglas!' Mom said.

'Only joking . . .'

'Your turn, Fanny,' Daddy said.

'I should know?'

'Your turn, Lou . . .' Daddy said and Sally could see how much he was enjoying his game.

'I'm afraid to even think about what you've got up your sleeve this time . . .'

'Aha . . .' Daddy looked around the table slowly, a smile spreading across his face. 'How about a ride in the Goodyear Blimp?'

'The Goodyear Blimp!' Douglas said, knocking over his dish of tapioca pudding.

'Twenty minutes over scenic Miami,' Daddy said.

'Hot dog!' Douglas said. 'That's what I've been wanting to do more than anything!'

'I know,' Daddy said. 'You've only mentioned it three or four hundred times.'

'Hot dog!' He slapped his thigh under the table. 'The Goodyear Blimp . . . wait till I tell Darlene.'

'Would you like to bring her along?'

'Would I? Oh, boy, Dad . . . you're the greatest . . . you think of everything!'

Sally, trying to match Douglas's enthusiasm, jumped up and down in her seat, saying, 'Hot dog . . . the Goodyear Blimp . . . wowie!' But the idea of it frightened her. She liked watching it, but riding in it was something else.

'Would you like to bring a friend, too?' Daddy asked her.

'Oh, sure . . . that's great . . . boy, am I excited!'

'Do you think it's a wise idea, Arnold?' Mom asked. 'After all . . . remember *The Hindenburg* . . .'

'This is 1948, Lou . . . besides, the Goodyear Blimp runs on helium, not hydrogen.'

'Some difference!' Mom said.

'There is.'

'Not to me.'

'That's because you don't understand the scientific facts, Mom . . .' Douglas said. 'I'll explain them to you. You see, the . . .'

Mom held up her hand. 'You know I have no head for science,' she said.

'Is it expensive?' Sally asked her father.

'About ten dollars a person . . .'

'Then I guess I'll invite Barbara,' Sally said, thinking out loud, 'because Andrea's father can afford to take her . . . and Shelby's grandmother probably wouldn't let her go anyway . . .'

'And I wouldn't blame her one bit,' Mom said.

'How about you, Fanny,' Daddy asked, ' . . . going to give it a try?'

'Ha ha,' Ma Fanny said, 'such a comedian! I like my feet on the ground.'

'How about you, Lou?' Daddy asked.

'No thank you!'

244

'Come on, Mom,' Douglas said. 'Live it up for once.'

'Remember, you enjoyed Cuba,' Daddy reminded her.

'I was very lucky,' Mom said. 'My first plane trip was a good one . . . let's just leave it at that . . .'

'I'd really like you to come with us,' Daddy said.

Sally looked from one to the other.

'I am *not* setting foot in that blimp,' Mom said, 'and I wish you'd have discussed the whole idea with me before you went ahead and told the children . . . after all, they're mine, too . . . don't I have anything to say about what happens to them?' She pushed her chair away from the table and ran for the bathroom.

Daddy cleared his throat.

Ma Fanny carried the pudding bowl back into the kitchen.

'Well . . .' Douglas said, 'I think I'll give Darlene a call and tell her the good news.'

Sally just sat there, watching, waiting and wondering.

'Would you like to take a little walk?' Daddy asked her.

'I have to call Barbara first . . .'

'You can call when we get back . . . Douglas is on the phone now.'

'Okay,' Sally said.

They went outside. It was just turning dark. The air was warm and sweet-smelling.

'Your mother worries a lot,' Daddy said, as they passed the goldfish pool.

Sally nodded.

'She can't help it . . . she loves us all so much . . . but I don't want you to grow up worrying that way.' He took her hand in his.

'Miss Swetnick is moving in there,' Sally said, pointing to the next building. 'Did I tell you I helped her and Hank paint their bathroom?'

'That's nice,' Daddy said, but Sally could tell he had something more serious on his mind. And it made her uncomfortable.

'Some people worry away their whole lives . . .' He looked down at her. 'Do you know what I mean?'

'I think so.'

'Your mother, for instance, spends too much time worrying about what *might* happen.'

'Why does she do that?'

'I don't know . . . that's just the way she is.'

'Don't you ever worry?' Sally asked.

'Sure . . . everybody worries sometimes . . . it's just that some people worry so much about tomorrow they have no time to enjoy today. Do you understand?'

'I think so.'

'You don't worry, do you?' Daddy asked.

'Well . . . only if it's very important . . .'

'At your age you should be free of worries.'

'There are some things I *have* to worry about.'

'I know,' he said, squeezing her fingers, 'spelling tests and boyfriends . . .'

She squeezed back without saying anything. How

could she tell him that *he* was the one she worried about most?

'I'm going to tell you a secret, Sally . . . I think you're ready to hear it . . . both of my brothers were exactly my age when they died . . .'

'They were?' Sally tried to sound surprised.

'Yes . . . your Uncle Eddie and your Uncle Abe . . . and I used to worry that the same thing would happen to me . . . that I would die when I was forty-two . . . and I didn't want to . . . I didn't want to leave you and Douglas and Mom . . .'

Sally tried to keep her breathing quiet, while inside she felt ready to explode.

'But now I realize how foolish it was for me to worry about that . . . because it was just a co-incidence . . . it has nothing to do with me. It's taught me something, though . . . I've learned what's really important . . . to experience everything that life has to offer . . . to be near the ones I love . . .' He looked down at her. 'Don't cry, Sally . . . don't, honey . . . I didn't mean to make you cry . . . stop now . . . stop, Sally . . .' He held her to him.

But Sally couldn't stop. It felt so good to let it all out. 'I don't want you to die,' she said, hugging her father.

'Everybody has to die, Sal . . .'

'Promise me you won't.'

'I can't promise that . . . we live and we die . . . it's a fact we have to accept . . .'

'But you won't die until I'm old, will you?'

'I hope not . . . but I'm not going to worry about it and I don't want you to either.'

When they went back upstairs, Douglas was sitting at the kitchen table, listening to *Inner Sanctum*. Ma Fanny was sitting in the stuffed chair in the living-room, working on a red sweater, and Mom was stretched out on the Murphy bed, holding a magazine upside down. The only sound in the apartment, besides the radio, was the click-clack of Ma Fanny's knitting needles.

Sally couldn't get to sleep. Couldn't stop thinking that one day *she* would be dead, too. What would it feel like? It could be nice. It could be that she'd turn into an angel and fly around and watch what was going on down on earth. Suppose she knew she was going to die in one month, like in that radio programme she'd heard last week. What would she do? See a lot of movies, for one thing. And eat whipped cream at every meal and have a party every week, with boys, and never do anything she didn't feel like doing. And she'd get a kitten. Maybe two or three of them. And she'd get all the cut-out books she wanted, and if Mrs Daniels said, *Cut-out books at her age? Why, when my Bubbles was her age she . . .* this time Sally wouldn't let her finish. She'd say, *I know all about your Bubbles . . . she did it with a goy and got a baby . . . so ha ha on you.*

And then she'd fly up to heaven and be a beautiful angel with long blonde hair. Or maybe she'd keep her own hair because who says angels can't have brown hair? But if it turned out that there were no angels and when you died there was nothing . . . because you were just plain dead . . . dead and cold . . . lying in the ground . . . *oh!* She moaned at the idea of that. There had to be angels. There just had to be!

TWENTY MINUTES OVER SCENIC MIAMI IN THE GOODYEAR BLIMP the sign said. They sat in a small compartment on the underside of the blimp: Sally and Barbara, Douglas and Darlene, Daddy and two strangers, who also had tickets for the 2 p.m. ride. Sally was scared and excited at the same time. So was Barbara. 'This could be it,' she said. 'We could crash during take-off . . . or burn up, like *The Hindenburg* . . .' She and Sally held hands. 'Do you believe in life after death?' Barbara asked.

'Yes . . . do you?'

'Today I do.'

'I believe in angels,' Sally said.

'Me too . . . Jewish angels,' Barbara said. 'Not the Christian kind who go around blowing bugles.'

'Right,' Sally said. 'Jewish angels . . .' It had never occurred to her that angels had to be one religion or the other.

Suddenly they lifted up . . . up, up, into the sky. They were floating. And down below them was scenic Miami and the Atlantic Ocean. It was fun looking down. Scary but fun. Everything seemed so small.

Darlene and Douglas talked on and on about

249

helium and how it works and that it was too bad the U.S. government wasn't smart enough to build lots of blimps. And that some day the two of them would build their own and possibly start a magazine called *Blimp News*.

Daddy looked across the compartment at Sally and smiled. She smiled back and let go of Barbara's hand. Her own was all sweaty.

When they were down again, when the ride was over, Barbara leaned close to Sally and whispered, 'I don't believe in angels after all. When you're dead, you're dead, and that's it.'

Chapter 25

Sally was home with Ma Fanny. Douglas and Mom and Daddy had gone to Lincoln Road to buy a suit for Douglas because Darlene had invited him to her house for dinner and Mom said *The Swells* dress up when they eat.

Sally had the phone to her ear. Ma Fanny knew she listened in to other people's conversations but she never told on her.

'Papa . . . Papa is that you?' A woman's voice asked.

'It's me,' Mr Zavodsky answered.

'Oh, I'm so glad you got a phone . . . I worry about you . . .'

'Don't worry . . . I couldn't be better.'

'Papa, I wish you'd come to live with us . . . Murray wants you and so do the boys. We'd fix up the attic room so you'd have privacy . . .'

'I like it here, Rita . . . who needs the cold?'

'Are you still having pains?'

'Not a one.'

'That's wonderful! And you're going to the doctor?'

'When I feel like it.'

'But Papa, you're supposed to go every two weeks . . .'

'You shouldn't worry, Rita . . . I'm fine . . . I'm enjoying . . .'

'That's good. You take care of yourself . . . promise?'

'I promise . . . I promise . . .'

'I'll call you again in a few weeks.'

'Did Hitler have any kids?' Sally asked that night.

'Not that I know of,' Mom said. 'And what's this sudden fascination with Hitler?'

'I'm just trying to get the facts straight,' Sally said. 'Was he married?'

'He had a girl-friend,' Mom said.

'Was her name Rita?'

'No . . . Eva.'

'Oh, Eva.'

So . . . the phone conversation had been in code again, Sally thought. He didn't have a daughter. And Rita was probably Eva. And they were making plans. And Murray and the boys were probably his old cronies, like Simon. Too bad the police weren't smart enough to crack Mr Zavodsky's code.

Douglas was angry. He'd worn his new suit to Darlene's house for dinner and Darlene's father had worn a golf shirt and Darlene's brothers had worn bathing suits and Darlene's mother had worn a bathrobe – a pretty fancy one, but still a bathrobe – and Darlene had worn dungarees and sneakers. 'Only the maid was dressed up,' Douglas told them.

'How was I to know *The Swells* have no manners?' Mom asked.

'They have manners,' Douglas said. 'They say *please*

and *thank you* and all that and they were really nice to me. Her father even offered me a tee shirt.'

'Next time you'll know better,' Daddy said. 'But your mother was right to want you to make a good impression . . . not just on them, but on everyone.'

'Yeah . . . sure . . .' Douglas answered.

Sally and Barbara were hot from playing statues in Sally's side yard. They lay down under the trees to rest. Across the yard, Ma Fanny and some of her friends were talking and knitting.

'Miss Swetnick's getting married tomorrow,' Sally said.

'I know.'

'I wish we could go to the wedding . . . she probably wanted to invite the whole class but there wasn't enough room.'

'Probably . . .' Barbara said. She rolled a coconut toward Sally. 'We could go to the temple and stand outside . . . you don't have to be invited for that . . .'

'And see her dressed as a bride?' Sally sat up.

'Sure.'

'Let's do it!' Sally rolled the coconut back to Barbara.

'Okay . . . and I know something else we could do at the same time.'

'What?'

'Kiss Peter,' Barbara said.

'*You* want to kiss Peter?'

'No . . .' Barbara said, 'I mean you . . . *you* could kiss him.'

'Who says I want to?'

'Don't you?'

'Well . . . I wouldn't mind . . . but not in front of a lot of people.'

'We'll get him away from the people.'

'How?'

'Oh . . . we'll say you have a surprise for him or something.'

'And you'll do all the talking?' Sally asked.

'Sure . . . all you'll have to say is *congratulations* . . . and then kiss him . . . it'll be easy . . . everybody kisses at weddings.'

'I don't know . . .'

'If you don't want to . . .' Barbara began.

'It's not that . . .'

' . . . or if you're *chicken* . . .'

'I'm *not* chicken!'

'Then it's all set,' Barbara said, standing up. She brushed off her hands. 'I'll meet you at the corner at noon . . . and Sally . . .'

'What?'

'Don't wear your hair in braids . . . let it hang loose for a change.'

Sally and Barbara stood outside Temple Beth-El, waiting. Each of them had a bag of rice. It was very hot and Sally wore her new off-the-shoulder midriff. She had a hibiscus tucked behind one ear and her hair hung loose, below her shoulders. She checked herself in the mirror and was surprised that she looked so much like Lila. When Miss Swetnick and

Hank came out of the temple everyone cheered and threw rice. Miss Swetnick looked beautiful but she wasn't wearing her glasses and Sally could tell that she was having some trouble without them by the way she squinted at the crowd. She laughed as she tossed her bouquet. Sally hoped to catch it but Miss Swetnick aimed it at her bridesmaids. Then she and Hank got into a shiny car and drove away.

Peter was wearing the same kind of blue suit that Douglas had worn to *The Swells'* house for dinner, but he had already loosened his tie and unbuttoned his shirt collar.

'So, Petey . . .' a fat, older woman said, 'you're next?'

'Like fish!' Peter told her.

Sally and Barbara went over to him. 'Hi, Peter . . .'

Barbara said, 'Sally has something for you.'

Peter said, 'Oh, yeah . . . what?'

Barbara said, 'Something she can only give you in private.'

Peter said, 'Okay . . . let's have it.'

Barbara said, 'Over there . . .' And she nudged Sally toward the side yard of the temple. 'Come on, Peter . . . or you'll never find out what it is.'

It was too late to back out now. She never should have come to the wedding. She never should have let Barbara get things going.

When the three of them reached the side yard Peter said, 'Okay . . . we're in private now.'

'Well . . .' Sally said, taking a deep breath, 'in

honour of your brother's wedding, congratulations!'
She leaned over and kissed him on the mouth.

He turned bright red. 'What'd you do that for?'

Sally blushed too. 'I told you . . . it was in honour
of your brother's wedding . . .' She chewed on her
bottom lip and pulled at her midriff.

Peter leaned over and kissed Sally back.

'What's *that* for?' she asked.

'For letting me copy off you on our last spelling
test.'

'Petey . . . hurry . . .' the fat woman called.

'See you,' Peter said, running off.

'See you . . .' Sally called, waving.

'Well . . .' Barbara said. 'You really did it!'

'Uh huh . . .'

'Tell me about it.'

'You were standing right here,' Sally said. 'You saw
the whole thing.'

'But what did it *feel* like?' Barbara asked.

'Nice.'

'I always knew he liked you.'

'I wish Jackie knew it.'

'She will . . .'

When Sally got back to her house there was an
ambulance and a police car outside and a crowd of
people standing around. Oh no . . . Sally thought,
please God . . . don't let it be Doey . . . She pushed
her way into the crowd. He's going to be all right . . .
he promised . . .

'Let me in . . . let me in . . .' Sally said, using her

elbows. The hibiscus fell from behind her ear and she tramped over it. 'Everybody has to die . . .' she could hear her father saying. 'We live and we die . . .' 'But you won't die until I'm old, will you?' she asked. And he had answered, 'I hope not . . .' She forced her way through until she reached the front of the crowd.

Andrea was there. 'Did you hear the news?'

'No . . . what?' Please God . . . please . . .

'It's Mr Zavodsky . . .'

Sally felt dazed, as if she might pass out.

'You know . . .' Andrea added, 'that old guy who gives us candy . . .'

'What about him?' Sally asked. So, the police had found out on their own . . .

'He's dead!' Andrea said.

'He can't be.'

'Well, he is. He had a heart attack on the stairs. He just keeled right over . . . my grandmother's friend found him and called the ambulance. They're bringing him out any second . . . I'm not going to look . . . are you?'

'Yes!' Sally said. Thank you, God . . . Thank you for not letting it be Doey . . .

'There . . .' Andrea pointed and started sniffling, as two attendants carried out a stretcher.

'How can you cry?' Sally asked. 'You should be glad it's him and not . . . not . . .'

'He was a little touched,' Andrea said, 'but he was nice . . .'

'That's how much you know!'

'Poor Mr Zavodsky . . .' Andrea cried, 'all covered up with a blanket . . .'

'I have to go now . . .' Sally said. 'I'll see you later.' She walked away slowly, through the lobby, up the stairs, to her apartment. She pulled her keepsake box out from under the day bed, opened it, rummaged through the shells, marbles, withered flowers, notes from Peter, and letters from Daddy, and fished out her Hitler letters, including the one she had written, but never mailed, to the Chief of Police.

She carried her letters back downstairs. The street was empty now, and quiet, except for a small group of old men and women, talking softly, where the crowd had stood a few moments before. She went to the trash bins, next to the storage room, and tore each letter into tiny pieces. So, it was over! She dropped them into the bin one by one. There was no more Mr Zavodsky. He was dead.

She sat down on the step. But maybe he's dead *not* from a heart attack! Maybe Simon and Rita murdered him. Yes, they'd found out someone was hot on his trail and the only thing to do was kill him to protect themselves! They'd injected poison, the kind that works fast and leaves no trace. And now Adolf would rot in hell. He'd shovel coal down there for a million years. He'd find out how it felt to get shoved into an oven, like Lila. God would see to that!

Douglas rode up on his bicycle, finished exploring for the day.

'Mr Zavodsky's dead!' Sally told him.

'Who's he?'

'Oh Douglas . . . don't you have any imagination?' Sally stood up and walked away.

Chapter 26

June 10, 1948

Dear Chrissy,
I'm coming home soon. My father is driving down next week and then we are going to take the scenic route back to New Jersey. We will visit St Augustine, Bok Tower, Silver Springs and other exciting places in Florida that I have studied about this year. You probably never heard of any of them. We will wind up in Washington, D.C. where I will inspect the FBI, as I am thinking seriously of joining it.

As soon as I get home I'm planning on having a party. I may or may not invite boys. I may or may not invite Alice Ingram, since I haven't heard from her once. Have you grown any this year? I've hardly grown at all. Not up and not out, either. But I have learned a lot. Do you know the difference between helium and hydrogen? Do you know how babies get made? Have you kissed any boys? I have. I will tell you about that too. It's more interesting than the difference between helium and hydrogen. Have you heard about television? My father says we are going to get a set when we get home. You can come over to watch. My father says it's going to be a big thing. My mother says nothing will ever replace the radio. I am in-between my mother and my father, not just about television, but about a lot of things. That is something else I've found out this year.

Well, see you soon. Don't do anything I wouldn't do.
Love and other indoor sports,
Sally F.

Sally was packing a carton with Crayolas, books, her keepsake box and her toe slippers.

'And when we get home . . .' Douglas was saying, tying up his carton, 'I want you to stay away from Union Woods.'

'I'm not the one who plays in Union Woods,' Sally said, trying to decide on whether or not to pack her Margaret O'Brien paper dolls.

'I mean it . . . you stay out of there,' Douglas said.

'I will . . . I will . . .'

'Because some really bad things could happen to you in Union Woods . . .'

'I know . . . I could trip jumping across the brook and dislocate my elbow and wind up with a kidney infection and then . . .'

'That's not exactly how it happened,' Douglas said, interrupting.

'It's not?'

'No . . .'

'How did it happen then?'

'If you could keep a secret I'd tell you.'

'I can . . . I can . . . I've finally learned . . .'

'How can I be sure?' Douglas asked. 'How do I know I can really trust you this time?'

'You can, Douglas . . . I swear it . . . I've changed a lot.'

261

'Since when?'

'Since that time about *The Outlaw* . . .'

'Well . . .'

'Oh, come on, Douglas . . . I'll tell you a secret too.'

'Okay,' Douglas said. 'You go first.'

'I kissed Peter Hornstein on the lips . . . and that's a real secret because if Mom ever found out she'd kill me . . . a person could get trench mouth that way, or worse . . .'

Douglas laughed.

'It's not funny.'

'Trench mouth . . .' He rolled around on the floor, laughing and holding his stomach. 'You're so dumb . . . you believe everything Mom tells you.'

'I do not!'

'Name one thing she's told you that you don't believe . . .'

'I don't believe my fungus came from the living-room rug.'

This made Douglas laugh harder.

'Stop it!' Sally said. 'You promised to tell me your secret . . .'

Douglas lay flat on his back, panting. 'Okay . . . the real reason I was running in Union Woods . . .' He paused.

'Go on . . . go on . . .'

'It was the crazy guy.'

'What crazy guy?'

'You know . . . the one who hangs out in the woods . . .'

'You mean the one they warned us about in school . . . the *crazy* one?'

Douglas nodded. 'That's what I just said . . . he was chasing us . . .'

'Oh, Douglas . . . that's so exciting! Could you identify him for the police?'

'I'm not sure.'

'Did he, by any chance, have a small black moustache?'

'Why . . . do you think he was Hitler?' Douglas doubled up with laughter. Sally had never seen him this way.

'It's not funny!'

'It is . . . it is . . . Hitler in Union Woods . . .'

'Stop it, Douglas!'

'I can't . . . I can't . . . it's just too much . . .'

Sally started laughing too. She couldn't help it either. It *was* funny . . . *Hitler in Union Woods* . . . why would he bother to go there? 'You know something, Douglas . . . when we get home I'm going to give you a special name, like I did for Doey-bird and Ma Fanny . . .'

'That's really big of you, Sally . . . but if you don't mind I think I'll just stick with plain old Douglas . . . that's good enough for me.'

'If I didn't know better I'd take that as an insult.'

'Insult . . . schminsult,' Douglas said, and he stood up, still laughing, and headed for the bathroom.

Sally leaned back against the day bed, holding her

Margaret O'Brien paper dolls. Just one more story before I finish packing, she thought. Yes, this will be a good one. I'll call it *Margaret O'Brien Meets the Crazy One.*

JUDY BLUME

BLUBBER

It's easy to laugh, but what happens
when the joke's on you?

When pudgy Linda is given the cruel name of
Blubber by her classmates, Jill laughs along with
everyone else. It's easier that way, right? It's not
until Jill becomes a victim of bullying herself that
she realizes how much it hurts and how hard it
can be to stand up for yourself.

Turn the page to read an extract

'It's very foolish to laugh if you don't know what's funny in the first place.'

My best friend, Tracy Wu, says I'm really tough on people. She says she wonders sometimes how I can like her. But we both know that's a big joke. Tracy's the best friend I'll ever have. I just wish we were in the same fifth-grade class.

My teacher is Mrs Minish. I'm not crazy about her. She hardly ever opens the windows in our room because she's afraid of getting a stiff neck. I never heard anything so dumb. Some days our room gets hot and stuffy and it smells – like this afternoon. We'd been listening to individual reports on The Mammal for almost an hour. Donna Davidson was standing at the front of the room reading hers. It was on the horse. Donna has this *thing* about horses.

I tried hard not to fall asleep but it wasn't easy. For a while I watched Michael and Irwin as they passed a *National Geographic* back and forth. It was open to a page full of naked people. Wendy and Caroline played Tic-Tac-Toe behind Wendy's notebook. Wendy won three games in a row. I wasn't surprised. Wendy is a very clever person. Besides being class president, she is also

3

group science leader, recess captain and head of the goldfish committee.

Did Mrs Minish notice anything that was going on or was she just concentrating on Donna's boring report? I couldn't tell from looking at her. She had a kind of half-smile on her face and sometimes she kept her eyes closed for longer than a blink.

To make the time go faster I thought about Hallowe'en. It's just two days away. I love to dress up and go Trick-or-Treating, but I'm definitely not going to be a dumb old witch again this year. Donna will probably be a horse. She dresses up like one every Hallowe'en. Last year she said when she grows up she is going to marry a horse. She has him all picked out and everything. His name is San Salvador. Most of the time Donna smells like a horse but I wouldn't tell her that because she might think it's a compliment.

I yawned and wiggled around in my chair.

'In closing,' Donna said, 'I would like you to remember that even though some people say horses are stupid that is a big lie! I personally happen to know some very smart horses. And that's the end of my report.'

The whole class clapped, not because Donna's report was great, but because it was finally over. Mrs Minish opened her eyes and said, 'Very nice, Donna.'

Earlier, when I had finished my report on the lion, Mrs Minish said the same thing to me. *Very nice, Jill*. Just like that. Now I couldn't be sure if she really meant it. My report wasn't as dull as Donna's but it wasn't as long either. Maybe the longer you talk the better grade you get. That wouldn't be fair though. Either way, I'm glad Mrs Minish calls on us alphabetically and that my last name is Brenner. I come right after Bruce Bonaventura.

Mrs Minish cleared her throat. 'Linda Fischer will give the last report for today,' she said. 'We'll hear five more tomorrow and by the middle of next week everyone will have had a turn.'

I didn't think I'd be able to live through another report.

'Are you ready, Linda?' Mrs Minish asked.

'Yes,' Linda said, as she walked to the front of the room. 'My report is uh . . . on the whale.'

Caroline and Wendy started another game of Tic-Tac-Toe while Bruce went to work on his nose. He has a very interesting way of picking it. First he works one nostril and then the other and whatever he gets out he sticks on a piece of yellow paper inside his desk.

The hand on the wall clock jumped. Only ten minutes till the bell. I took a piece of paper out of my desk to keep a record of how many times Linda said *And uh* . . . while she gave her report. So far I'd counted seven. Linda's head is shaped like a potato and sits right on her shoulders as if she hasn't got any neck. She's also the pudgiest girl in our class, but not in our grade. Ruthellen Stark and Elizabeth Ryan are about ten times fatter than Linda, but even they can't compare to Bruce. If we had a school fat contest he would definitely win. He's a regular butterball.

'Blubber is a thick layer of fat that lies under the skin and over the muscles of whales,' Linda said. 'And uh ... it protects them and keeps them warm even in cold water. Blubber is very important. Removing the blubber from a whale is a job done by men called flensers. They peel off the blubber with long knives and uh ... cut it into strips.' Linda held up a picture. 'This is what blubber looks like,' she said.

Wendy passed a note to Caroline. Caroline read it, then turned around in her seat and passed it to me. I unfolded it. It said: *Blubber is a good name for her!* I smiled, not because I thought the note was funny, but because Wendy was watching me. When she turned away I crumpled it up and left it in the corner of my desk. The next thing I knew, Robby Winters, who sits next to me, reached out and grabbed it.

Linda kept talking. 'And uh ... whale oil is obtained by heating the blubber of the whale. European margarine companies are the chief users of whale oil and uh ... it also goes into glycerine and some laundry soaps and has other minor uses. Sometimes Eskimos and Japanese eat blubber ...'

When Linda said that Wendy laughed out loud and once she started she couldn't stop. Probably the reason she got the hiccups was she laughed too hard. They were very loud hiccups. The kind you can't do anything about.

Pretty soon Robby Winters was laughing too.

He doesn't laugh like an ordinary person – that is, no noise comes out. But his whole body shakes and tears run out of his eyes and just watching him is enough to make anybody start in, so the next minute we were all roaring – all except Linda and Mrs Minish. She clapped her hands and said, 'Exactly what is going on here?'

Wendy let out a loud hiccup.

Mrs Minish said, 'Wendy, you are excused. Go and get a drink of water.'

Wendy stood up and ran out of the room.

By then Wendy's note about Blubber had travelled halfway around the class and I couldn't stop laughing, even when Mrs Minish looked right at me and said, 'Jill Brenner, will you please explain the joke.'

I didn't say anything.

'Well, Jill . . . I'm waiting . . .'

'I don't know the joke,' I finally said, finding it hard to talk at all.

'You don't know why you're laughing?' Mrs Minish asked.

I shook my head.

'It's very foolish to laugh if you don't know what's funny in the first place.'

I nodded.

'If you can't control yourself you can march straight to Mr Nichols' office and explain the situation to him.'

I nodded again.

'I'm waiting for your answer, Jill.'

'I forgot the question, Mrs Minish.'

'The question is, can you control yourself?'

'Oh . . . yes, Mrs Minish . . . I can.'

'I hope so. Linda, you may continue,' Mrs Minish said.

'I'm done,' Linda told her.

'Well . . . that was a very nice report.'

The bell rang then. We pushed back our chairs and ran for the row of lockers behind our desks. Mrs Minish has to dismiss us at exactly two thirty-five. Otherwise we'd miss our buses.

It's very important to get on the right one. On the first day of school my brother, Kenny, got on the wrong bus and wound up all the way across town. Since my mother and father were both at work the principal of Long-meadow School had to drive Kenny home. I would never make such a mistake. My bus is H-4. That means Hillside School, route number four. I'm glad Kenny doesn't go to my school. Next year he will, but right now he is just in fourth grade and only fifth and sixth graders go to Hillside.

When I got on the bus Tracy was saving me a seat. Caroline and Wendy found two seats across from us. Before this year I'd never been in either one of their classes but this is my second time with Linda Fischer and I've been with Donna, Bruce and Robby since kindergarten.

'We had the best afternoon,' Tracy said. 'Mr Vandenburg invented this game to help us get our multiplication facts straight and I was *forty-eight* and every time he called out *six times eight* or *four times twelve* I had to jump up and yell *Here!* It was so much fun.'

'You're lucky to be in his class,' I said. 'I wish he'd give Mrs Minish some ideas.'

'She's the wrong type.'

'You're telling me!'

As Linda climbed on to the bus Wendy shouted, 'Here comes Blubber!' And a bunch of kids called out, 'Hi, Blubber.'

Our bus pulled out of the driveway and as soon as we turned the corner and got going Robby Winters sailed a paper airplane down the aisle. It landed on my head.

'Pass it here, Jill,' Wendy called. When I did, she whipped out a magic marker and wrote *I'm Blubber – Fly Me* on the wing. Then she stood up and aimed the plane at Linda.

The group of girls who always sit in the last row of seats started singing to the tune of 'Beautiful Dreamer', *Blubbery blubber . . . blub, blub, blub, blub . . .*

At the same time, the airplane landed on two sixth-grade boys who ripped it up to make spit balls. They shot them at Linda. Then Irwin grabbed her jacket off her lap. 'She won't need a coat this winter,' he said. 'She's got her blubber to keep her warm.' He tossed the jacket up front and we played Keep-Away with it.

'Some people even eat blubber!' Caroline shrieked, catching Linda's jacket. 'She said so herself.'

'Ohhh . . . disgusting!' Ruthellen Stark moaned, clutching her stomach.

'Sick!'

The girls in the back started their song again. *Blubbery blubber . . . blub, blub, blub, blub . . .*

The bus driver yelled, 'Shut up or I'll put you all off!'

Nobody paid any attention.

Linda picked the spit balls out of her hair but she still didn't say anything. She just sat there, looking out the window.

When we reached the first stop Wendy threw Linda's jacket to me. She and Caroline ran down the aisle and as Linda stood up, Wendy called back, 'Bye, Blubber!'

Linda stopped at my row. I could tell she was close to crying because last year, when Robby stepped on her finger by mistake, she got the same look on her face, right before the tears started rolling.

'Oh, here,' I said and I tossed her the jacket. She got off and I saw her race down the street away from Wendy and Caroline. They were still laughing.

I—just to go here turned over to...

... too harder. "Eyes see..." The third...

... darker, which, sort of... I think, the...

the sill.

... I said to her that...

I remarked the satisfaction of her cry. She
one sort didn't say anything. She still sat there
staring out the window.

Presently we reached the part that crosses close
to—but I can't tell the full story now. I'll finish
the saga. Just as I knew I could, I'd done it.
For Ego Bippot.

I stopped at a moment. I could feel she was
close to saying something, but I went on. I
dragged on her finger by finger. She felt the
same look on her face, which cleared the next
second falling.

"Yes, Love," I said and I looked her in the eye.
She got off and I saw life ripple down the street.
I was Dr. of Wendy, and I thought I was here and
the thinnest.

JUDY BLUME

IGGIE'S HOUSE

Not everything is as simple as black and white.

Winnie misses her best friend Iggie so much, but she's excited to meet the new family on the street, who are moving into Iggie's old house. Except the Garber family are black and there are some people on Grove Street who don't want them living there. Winnie is shocked by her neighbours' attitude, but making herself heard is proving difficult . . .